OUT OF CANAAN

OUT OF
CANAAN

KEITH A. RICE

Charles Scribner's Sons • New York

Copyright © 1983 Keith A. Rice

Library of Congress Cataloging in Publication Data

Rice, Keith A.
  Out of Canaan.
  I. Title.
  PS3568.I28708   1983   813'.54   82-23173
  ISBN 0-684-17857-5

1 3 5 7 9 11 13 15 17 19 F/C 20 18 16 14 12 10 8 6 4 2

Printed in the United States of America.

FOR
Juanita Gore

THE FAMILY

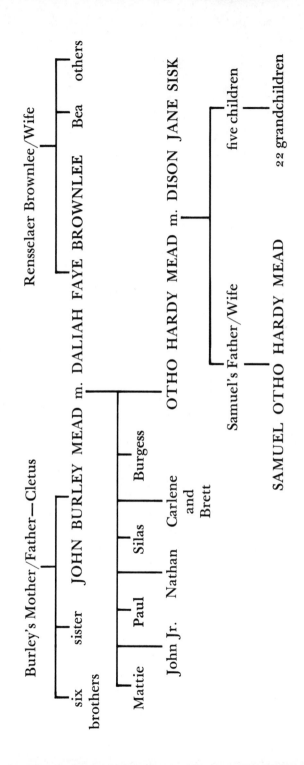

Burley's Mother/Father—Cletus

six brothers   sister   JOHN BURLEY MEAD m. DALIAH FAYE BROWNLEE

Rensselaer Brownlee/Wife

Bea   others

Mattie   Paul   Nathan   Silas   Carlene and Brett   Burgess

John Jr.

OTHO HARDY MEAD m. DISON JANE SISK

Samuel's Father/Wife

five children

SAMUEL OTHO HARDY MEAD

22 grandchildren

CHAPTER ONE

NOVEMBER

1963

SAMUEL THOUGHT, *I have the letter. I already have the letter from her hand.* And it was a fair hand, he imagined, too, looking long at the family photographs and the one gray-shaded Brownie frame, where among a gathering his Great-Grandmother Daliah was white powdered like the moon, or like the pale locust blossoms crushed into a mulch that his grandmother, Dison Jane, used on her flowers.

Otho leaned over him already speaking of times seldom hinted at, little cared about anymore, speaking loudly and maliciously because what the old man said was like rust and as foreign and unnerving as dust motes in sunlight. The grandson, Samuel Otho Hardy Mead, leaned far backward, sitting on the cane chair, as his grandfather leaned toward him—the angle equal, so that if the old man leaned any farther forward the grandson would have fallen backward into the curios and old leathers.

Samuel already knew, too, that Daliah Faye Brownlee Mead had been bedded by a southern millionaire out of state and come home with a child who, in his old age, was now asking him to listen. So Samuel was not surprised to hear when it was said.

"You could be a bastard too."

The grandfather rocked forward again, and stayed, speaking loudly over his deafness and ill-fitting teeth.

[3]

He laid a hand on Samuel's knee. His other hand fluttered for a moment, then came to rest above Samuel's right ear. It was as if Otho brought Samuel's eyes in line with his own to say more.

"Boy, I need to have you know these things. I have twenty-three grandbabies. You're not the oldest. Grace and Marshall's oldest daughter is seventeen, a year older than you. But I can't give this to my pretty girl. She's not thinking about family other than to marry in a few years."

"Carol is too busy placing things in a hope chest," Samuel said. His cousin Carol was a favorite. Samuel no longer was jealous she was the first grandchild.

"Oh, and yes," Otho said, "and you and I have a different kind of hope."

Samuel smiled. Otho's hand in his hair was warm like a first fishing hat. In fact, his grandfather had bought him his first. When Otho had given Samuel the hat, their second fishing of the Pond River together, Carol had been the jealous one then.

Otho took the clock from the shelf and wound it. He set the clock back. He spit again. "Thou shalt not commit adultery. God's Bible says such. Do you know what adultery is?"

Samuel almost came down out of his chair, bringing his feet flat, which catapulted the cane upright, propelling his face close against the old man's words, the sound hanging hard and prismatic.

"Good. I shocked you." Otho laughed. "No, boy, I mean the whole Mead family."

Samuel nodded.

"I was born mid-December 14, 1892. It's writ as such in our Bible." The old man turned his hands over, calloused and large, fumbling with an imaginary pen. "I was not born to home, not born in this state. I was born in Florida." He stopped writing. "Was near four months before I was legal in this family, written in our book so to speak. Papa did not know me, did not claim onto me. I believe it was because I was the charm. I am the seventh son of a seventh son."

Samuel did not speak. To speak would have displaced the dream. He saw the man's mouth move, saw the words materialize in the air—a farmhouse, a cemetery, a river ("He did say Salt River?"), and a great-faced man riding fast upon a mule, speaking down to a woman, small, delicate boned, and yet fierce. And the other children, the first six sons who the grandfather ticked off with his hands, the six names recorded above his own, laying a name at each fingertip, then the two daughters, and finally the old man's own name, Otho Hardy Mead, there at his right forefinger, which left the empty thumb strutting high and jerking toward the closet door behind Samuel's head.

The man brought down his thumb. "I have kept many things. How else can a man lay claim to what he is? I saved the photographs and the keepsakes to parade them before my sons and grandsons. I want to show you them. I want you to remember my story. Even if Dison would have you remember differently. If you and I are to pass the hope between us, I got to have you know I love all my grandchildren—but I love you the best."

Samuel thought, *He doesn't know I have it. He doesn't know I've been tempted already.*

Samuel had the letter. He did not know how much more Otho could tell. Daliah's hand had formed the letter. His grandmother, Dison Jane, had given it to him that morning. He dismissed the name for it was addressed to no one in the family. The name was old and unfamiliar: Jaretta Chapel—sounded high-reeling and preaching like a deacon's wife in a country church.

EARLIER THAT MORNING, JUST AFTER HE HAD RIDDEN his bike up to the porch, and come into the kitchen, ill-lit and cold because the fire had burned down, Dison Jane had laid kindling high on the left side of the stove to bank the coals. The smells of fried fats, peppers, and orange ring cake had hung bittersweet, and when the fire was allowed to go out, the orange-colored odor wedded the air. But today the room was November gray, and without the promise of sun. Dison's back was bent from him, so he saw only her legs beneath a dull skirt and the near-white knob at the top of her head. When let down her hair reached her waist. It had never been cut.

Dison Jane turned and he saw her face, washed and ash-colored, lined at the corners of her mouth and gathered in pleats around her throat. Her skin was less like china than earthenware or crockery. Being a good Christian her skin knew no powders, her lips no paints.

"Biscuits and syrup and butter under the cloth. Them eggs were rock a half hour ago. I threw them out," she said.

As he ate she continued around the kitchen. She cleaned the remaining flour from the high white sideboard, scraping it into a pile and over the side of the pullout workboard to cascade into the drawer below and its sifter. A white shower. High above the floor behind engraved and red-painted glass doors, among the glassware and cutlery, were her surprises: chewing gum, soft peppermint, and extra roll caps for her grandsons' toy pistols.

The butter and syrup rose between the tines of his fork. He scraped the mass onto a hard biscuit. She waited on the other side of the table, resting her old-age paunch against the back of the chair. He ate slowly, thinking about the eggs he had missed.

"Myself? I doubt she loved her husband. When she died, on the stone it read Daliah Faye Brownlee Mead like her maiden name was needed, was cared for the most to take to eternity. Hardly was room on the stone for John's name. He died in 1926." She moved her hand over the table. "You want more syrup?"

"No, Ma'am," he said.

She laid her hand back over her apron pocket. It was the letter. She fingered it flat in her clothing, a small square packet. "In 1926 John Burley Mead was seventy-one. Died in the winter of a phlegm. I believe he was always something of a consumptive in his later years. Prone to lung sickness—like your grandpa and your daddy." He looked up.

"They say there's powers in a seventh son of a seventh son. I put no stock to it. He cured two wens I know of in his life. Nothing more. His daddy died when he was seventy-one. Otho needs to pass on what he figures now that he'll be seventy-one in December late. It's an omen to him. His daddy died a seventh son at seventy-one. He's afraid being a seventh son—well, you can't know about being old. Some desperation to it all, the passing."

He did not pay much attention as she continued to speak. A progression of epithets and scenes came, some familiar (*Yes, I have seen that road*, he thought. *Is that a real diamond Great-Aunt Carlene wears?*) and others familiar only because he was now hearing them, and telling created memory, and he guessed he understood all along.

". . . with vanity on their face. Women like her, a good Christian member of the Grace Church she pretended to be, with her white face. Daliah powdered herself white and sang in the choir. Had a beautiful voice they say, and beautiful voices wile on men. I fear she did such with John Burley. And from what I knowed it was more than voice that called her and scandalized her."

Vanity? he thought.

". . . likely she had it planned a long time, the chances weighted, though I came to believe it was not for her a big undertaking—a certain smallness, a minor thinking in her mind to up and quit her John and her children."

She sat to the table with him now, had pulled out the opposite chair and proffered her opinions over the jar of peppers, green tomato relish and honey with the comb left in. He spooned up the last of the syrup and butter. The biscuits had given out.

"I could find you a picture of Daliah with her face painted white. As the years came on her she powdered more, until the year she died she was a ghost. Think she found that vanity for sure on her trip—like she was on a vacation, or with a busload of Methodists heading south for a revival beside the river."

She had to move her stomach from the table to get at the letter. She held it in both hands as if she were not quite relinquished of the telling, as if once the letter passed her hands, her tongue would become mute, and sound would be rendered by the aged paper alone. She finally gave it up, laying it quickly on the covered table, address side up in front of him, and withdrew.

"All I have to recall her for you, to give you some fairness to the man Otho's telling." She smiled slightly. "He clouds her in his mind. He is Christian in his heart, but his memory is not the gospel."

"Yes, Ma'am," he said.

CHAPTER TWO

APRIL

1892

ALIAH WATCHED FOR HIM; COULD NOT SEE HIM moving under the strong Kentucky sun. If only he would come. She wiped her hands on the apron, to make him believe she was dutiful; not watching, not sitting with breath held and a packed satchel under the bed. *I'm not old yet,* she told herself. *I don't even look thirty yet.* She dropped her apron to cover her thighs again. *He is not coming. He would make me wait on him even to leave him.* She cocked her ear to one side to hear the near rumble of her children playing in the side yard. April window light was on her face.

Daliah's black hair was coiled above her ears. Because it was not Sunday, her combs were unmatched: a white-shell comb set above her left ear; above her right, a brown wooden comb was placed loose in the coil. With her hair pulled back, the sun fell full across her cheeks, her ears, and to the nape of her neck, making her head seem thrown forward, as if she was always following something. Her eyebrows were straight, no arch to them; therefore Daliah could never be surprised. Her neck was long, her eyes gray.

Her hands pulled the muslin in a ball. The needle bit her hand as she worked on the sheets. Marriage bit at her too. The day she married John Burley Mead, her father sat to her kitchen table—hers because she had cleared it, had cooked and set food there—with the gun in his hands, swabbing at it with the tail of his shirt. Tucked behind her combs she wore stephanotis in her hair and the white gloves Jaretta Chapel had loaned her. She had never worn dress gloves before and the linen was stiff and strange between her fingers. Her dress was brown. On her cheeks she lay a hint of white flour to dull her wind-burnt skin. As she passed the table he reached for her and placed a sad hand at her waist. He said, "I know little to the loving. But you'll have many children out of that arch." She knew he kneaded at her hips to see how wifely and strong she would be. "Let him have of you what he must. Men know so little else of you women, don't know above your womb beats a heart also. He'll know when the beating stops beneath his hands— like your Ma." "Don't," she said. "No, listen, girl. I know I've been less to you than to any of the others. You were here the longest after she died, while the rest rose out of my house and were gone. You doubled on the chores, until finally there was no one, and grief beside me here." He fumbled at the gun, laid it down, smeared and greased with fats. "Tell him it is a gift. Don't tell him it's my pride I give away. You thought it was my pride? It's only a gun and pride if any should have been in you. I'm sorry it was not." The room was dark, and his hand still patted at her waist. She powdered her face again, piling it higher and heavier after the tears had turned the original flour to mud.

She watched for her children now as she sewed by the window. She stopped to see Burgess as he rounded the corner pulling a rope after him; was surprised when the rope rounded the corner and there was nothing. She thought maybe it had broken, that something had been left behind, cheating her, showing nothing but frayed hemp and cleaved grass. Then she knew: nothing had been tied, that Burgess needed nothing but his rope.

The children came to the table in bunches or singly. Two and three or four had played washers together: Paul, Nathan, John Jr., Silas, and the two girls, Mattie and Carlene. Burgess, three years younger because the twins had been a burden, came last through the screen door.

She had the last muslin seamed and stepped over the rope where Burgess had left it in his sunset running —both ends empty; air bridged to air—and smoothed the linens over the wire fence to bleach in the dews. The daily additions along the wire were shaded and fading, a week's worth of dew-blanched sheets—sheets like the one she lay upon when Burley came to her that night.

Burley was tall, green-eyed, wore square-toed boots, and smelled of worn leather. In his nakedness she remembered again his ripe, fecund drowsing amid seamed muslin sheets. She saw him naked, felt the fine corn-silk hairs of his body, and in the darkness, knew his skin was white; only the arms and deep neck of his shirt were creased and burned brown. She remembered his dust, his unseen nakedness, which was the seed of his eight children.

She knew the quiet touch of his feet as they moved over. His bare feet came to her, between, and against, with their warm blood. He buried the parallel coming of her tears; she did not understand why she could still hear outside of her crying the noiseless breathing of her other children and the turning of child-body on bedsprings. The dry rustle of her bed as Burley rolled away repeated as she rose from the sheets . . .

. . . passed the sheets, layered and damp also, but

with dew. She folded them from the fence and left them in a neat pile at the well shed. The road was wide; she did not take it. It washed too straight and without color under the blanched moon. She left the road, crossing it in nine steps. She gave her feet to the stirred dust of the mule trace. The ageless barn rode up on her right. The moon reached her second hand between its boards, flickering, with a halo above the sagging roofline.

After a mile the tracks began. She walked them. They were something to follow. Under moonlight, empty grass flowed. No station was near, only a place to take on wood, and the train sat between the trees. She heard horses above hollow boards, and the smell of manure rose up behind the quiet odor of alfalfa and oats. A line of cattle cars stood back, spaced by one grain hopper from a Pullman at the train's end. A red-shaded lamp high on the right side of the Pullman threw light into the trees. Farther forward the tinder glow was vague in the dark. Floating on the left was the red pinpoint of a cigar.

"By yourself?" The man flicked the cigar away.

The satchel and arm swung away. He touched her shoulder.

"South," he said.

She looked at his smooth-shaved cheeks, then upward into his unseen eyes under fair brows. "I'm going south. You were following the tracks south."

She said, "South is fine."

"You have relatives down the line? Someone to meet you somewhere?"

"I have a sister in Indiana. He'll know right off—"

"Indiana's that way." He pointed back north up the tracks.

"I'm not for Indiana, I says." She looked north, then back to see around him. "What's south of here?"

"There's Tennessee for sure. Then Georgia. I'm going to Florida."

Noise mounted at the front of a train. "Florida!" she said.

A lantern swung out from the engine. "We're leaving." The train shuddered. "Give you a lift down the line?"

"No, I couldn't."

Animals kicked forward. He stepped to the first rung. "Just to the next station then." He reached for her hand. She did not take his. She tossed her bag up to the rear stoop and lifted herself as the train moved. Light spilled over her feet and the solid platform. She was not afraid. She sat on the wooden step-up by the rail. He laughed behind her.

"I'm all right."

"Not in the night air."

"I couldn't," she said, coming across the threshold and the bright light. "I couldn't," she repeated, taking in the Pullman's red carpet, and the cherry glow of the oil lamp, the leatherbound books, bronze horse, decanter, a pair of brass-colored riding boots tumbling from a corner. On the desk the yellow pages of ledgers were illuminated. Near the door he fought with his boots. He fell, unbalanced. Daliah caught a heel and pulled off his boot. He was just like Burley.

She did not know what to do with the boot. She picked up her satchel and, clutching it to her breast, looked to set them both down.

Even without his boots he was tall. His hands closed on the decanter.

"I don't drink," she said. The sofa was soft, made of horsehair and erect—like one she had seen once in a boardinghouse in Harrodsburg while Burley stood a line to pay taxes at the courthouse.

"Are you rich?" She rubbed the fine grain of the boot. "You have these rich things. You are a millionaire."

He handled a perfectly lined ledger. "The bank does these for me. I can't see more than four numbers at a time," he said. "Therefore, I don't carry more than thousands in my pockets; don't think of my worth as more than pockets full of thousands." He sat behind his desk with the ledgers and seals and wax. He drank a bourbon, had a second.

Suddenly they were at a station. The horses began again. The slow ride of trees came out of their blur, became motion made solid. Beyond the windows, buildings and fences slowed. There was a glow of station windows.

"I've never known a man who could afford more than a new hame, or a roll of fence wire."

He took his boot from her, her hands falling over themselves, rubbing at her pale and perfect fingers. "You are married," he said. "But you have no ring."

"Burley did not buy one."

On the other side people moved against yellow curtains. She felt shamed to have spoken outside of her outraged marriage, to have anyone hear, bobbing and leering into the glass.

"It was me who never wanted a ring," she said. He would know it was a lie. She gave him another. "I can't be getting off here. It's too close. I'm glad to be riding a bit farther with you."

CHATTANOOGA LAY FINE AND BRIGHT. NO MIST WAS ON the morning, no earth-sweat obscured the highlands that lifted Chattanooga over the Tennessee River. Daliah was at the window watching the city approach the train. She had not slept at all. He had offered her the compartment and bed, but she declined, saying manners would not allow her, and that since her marriage she had kept no man's bed but Burl's. The sofa had been fine— though she had little use of it, wanting to see from the darkness what she could only feel in the hum of the train.

"Have you ever been to Chattanooga?" he asked. Beside her, looking over her shoulder, he fastened the last button on his gray vest. He buttoned the bottom one, then unbuttoned it. He was not quite ordered, something disheveled was about him; perhaps the crease of his trousers was not as sharp as an iron could have made, his shirt collar not as straight as it could be. Something underneath. Daliah wanted to turn his collar. She raised her hand to smooth the linen. She stopped.

He did not notice her hesitation. "Chatt'nooga looks right fine," she said. The station loomed in the distance.

"Is Chattanooga far enough from Burt—no, it was Burley, wasn't it?"

"I don't know no one in Chatt'nooga."

"Do you have money?"

He wore a fine gray coat, his leathers were polished, and he was surrounded by objects any one of which was worth a year in her life. He must know she carried no money.

"I'll be waiting here for you."

"You're going on?"

"Chatt'nooga's not the end."

"I'm going to Tampa, I—" He finished fingering the lower button. "You're going all the way . . . to Florida?" he asked.

She took up her satchel.

"Make your mind, Mrs.—"

"Daliah. Daliah Faye Brownlee Me— Brownlee was my maid name."

"What makes you think I'll take you to Florida?"

"You got me to Chatt'nooga. Florida can't be much farther," she said.

"What do I tell people? It would be scandalous."

"How much more scandalous? I've ridden many miles through Tennessee with you—and in the dark, I mind you. You put me off here, you think the gossip would be any different than if I was for Florida with you? People might say one night was all you needed to compromise a woman, rather than you was well bred enough to take days to have your way—days and all the distance to Florida."

"You have this planned, do you?" he said. "How determined are you?"

"Burley don't even know what Florida is."

He set the hat at an angle. At once he was complete; that underneath movement quieted, and his clothing was placed and perfect. "'Does Daliah Faye Brownlee?'"

———

BROAD STREET WAS NOT THAT BROAD. THE NUMBERED blocks from the station were fronted with Greek Revival facades like the Tennessee Mercantile and Trust whose brass doors gave them passage. Daliah followed him into its atrium.

"Wait for me," he said.

A clerk said, "Good morning, Mr. Krasavage." Before an oak door a large man pumped his hand and said, "Cass, good to see you."

The sofa was floral and mutely trimmed. The rose satchel clashed. She waited again, sitting on a sofa while a man did his business. *Like for Burley again,* she thought. The chandeliers flickered between the ceiling fans, revolving slowly in their winds, just as they had when she waited for John Burley to pay taxes in Harrodsburg the first year of their marriage.

Then, the crystal had chattered as the boardinghouse matron lighted the candles among the prisms. Daliah sat among the quiets, the hush of ageless Michelin skirts, the house table lighted by afternoon-into-evening sun and the movement of the clock. As she finished the chandelier, the matron looked backward, frighteningly, at Daliah. Daliah tried to get up. Her pregnancy, her first at sixteen, was encumbering and slow assaulting. *Burley,* she thought. *Burley.* The courthouse sign read: HOURS 8:30 TO 5:00; SATURDAY 7:30 TO 4:00. She turned around between the columns at the top of the stile. Across the square, lights blinked on at the boardinghouse as the candles were lit in the wings and the dining room. The chandelier above the sitting room sofa blazed red behind the rose-colored arch over the door. She edged one step at a time down and through the canna-bordered walks. Light went out in stores about the square. On one side street the pale yellow boards of walks shone beneath sawdust and spittle. Saloon windows were grimy. Burley leaned against the bar. A hulk of a man leered a sickened face at the windows, stumbled through the doors, and vomited into the street at her feet. Burley stumbled out next, pulling the linings of his flannel pockets inside out under the blue lamps. He dropped a coin and reached for it, slipping and falling to his knees, then backward, drunk. He saw her. "You could have stayed to home," he said. She was down on her knees in stages, wiping at his face and the spittle at the corner of his mouth. He showed her his teeth, pushing her calico handkerchief away. "You could have stayed to home," he said. She left him sprawled on the boardwalk. The house matron was surprised to see her return. Daliah's dress was spotted; she reeked. Sitting on the sofa, hands folded, she waited in the swirling refraction of prism and candlelight. Later Burley came through the door. The lady tried to stop him. "That's my woman. She's got my child in 'er." The lady looked apologetic. Burley was too drunk to sit the wagon. She would have to drive them home. "Come here, Dali . . ."

CASLIN SQUEEZED HER SHOULDER. "COME, DALIAH."

"Florida?" she said.

"We'll have to spend the night."

"I haven't the money for hotel beds."

"You forget. You think I'm a millionaire."

Out of doors again, she followed behind him. The walk was short. They passed large shop windows, she stopping once to breathe over a green taffeta garment. The dress was high-waisted with a delicate bodice. The voile sleeves on the dress were lifted so the hands rose high above the headless mannequin, praying without bowed head, lifting hands unmatched by eyes to the heaven. Glass separated her from desire. She sighed and turned to see Krasavage watching her. Daliah lifted her bag to cover her worn bosom.

"It wouldn't fit," she said, and stepped beyond him. He walked at her elbow. He talked easily of other trips to Chattanooga. He looked over his shoulder once in his easy speech, trying to see the dress he had passed without notice.

"COME UP, HORSE," HE SAID. THE HORSE ROLLED THE CAR-
riage back. "I was in Chattanooga that September in '63.
I was thirteen, no fourteen, that year. I drove supply up
the valley of that creek." He remembered his youth.
"They call that creek Chickamauga! I was near a boy,
you see." He stopped a moment. "Fourteen."

Daliah sat with the noon sun on her head. He
pushed his hat back. He did not look like a soldier.

"I was no soldier. And there was this ridge."

They picnicked in an open meadow. He stood on a
corner of a red cloth; she laid out chicken and other
cold meats, great cloudlike biscuits—was surprised to
find assorted fruits out of season. The sun shone
through the wine. She cleared the trace of hotel dust.
The label said 1883. In 1883 she had birthed her fifth
child.

"Here, let me open it," he said.

He fumbled in the basket, brought out two
stemmed glasses, stood and poured. The same bite, yet
cleaner, not as fruity as fox grape wine, a light pale
vintage with a bouquet that rose above her accustomed
country sweet air of alfalfa and dog fennel. She drank
color. It was red like a December sun. *You have made
me drink wine that is not scuppernong. You can't see
wine as it ferments in its crock!*

His eyes were luminous under the trees. They sat
under the eaves of poplars and the grass flowed in a
wind passing through the meadow. He covered his eyes.
He blinded them to say the words in the dark. "I still
had the wagon, loaded with the wounded so bloody the
gray uniforms were maroon. A man leaned against my
back. He had no eyes. The blood and the retch were on

them, and the smell. I was fourteen that year, and it was cold that winter in North Georgia."

Wine burned in her stomach. She pushed the chicken closer. She wanted him to eat. She pushed the chicken closer again. He relented and fingered a white cut of breast, but laid it aside. He lay on his back and pulled the hat further over his eyes. Daliah stared off into the grass. She held the empty glass, did not see it, made her decision.

"This is a picnic," she said.

INTO THE BASIN THE WATER POURED CLEAR; THE PORCE-lain sang with hot scented waters, and as she splashed her face, blood was brought beneath her cheeks. When the pitcher was empty, she looked for more to find the hotel had drawn her a bath. The water was furious as she beat her fists against the pallid skim of soap: she stopped, knew she was envious of the man, afraid she drowned under his volume. "I want—" she said. She listened to herself speak and was not afraid. "I want like his." Her body spoke. It ached from wine. Rising wet and then standing before a full-length mirror, she tied the lacings of her chemise over her breasts. She pulled them tighter, lifting her form slightly. "I could be twenty-five," she said.

She lifted her hair, thought of placing it so, and dragged the bench in front of the mirror. As she raised her hair from her head, her long singing throat emerged, limber, delicately ligamented, and as she turned to see her small ears, the tendons drew tight, and the blood beat into the reflection of her skin. She whispered hymns.

She looked at his note again, humming. She had

received the letterhead through the door from a hotel maid. His handwriting strutted across the page, just like his ledgers. Perhaps he did know more of his worth than he had said.

She opened the rose-colored satchel. She pulled the dress over her head. It fell in place across her shoulders and breasts, and the last fall of material framed her feet. She pushed it down over her hips trying to wipe away some of the plainness. It was a church dress, linsey-woolsey, with an unadorned high collar. She had no jewelry (Caslin had said, "Not even a wedding band"). Beside the mirror was a low vase of spring violets. They were delicate, like her, and bringing a cluster to her hands, she placed three perfect flowers behind the combs in her hair. She had no perfume. From her bag came a leather pouch, white corn flour which she powdered on her face, making her pulled-back hair look more severe. "Maybe twenty-three," she said.

The lobby was a flood of people. Flowers were everywhere. Daliah hung back. The ladies in taffeta rustled. She was soundless in her worn spun cloth. No gloves, or ornaments; violets. *Wait,* she told herself. Solid movement surrounded her, carried her lightly behind men and women's vacated air; even now the air held vaporous among hotel lights the power of jasmine-scented waters, cigar smoke, and tweed. She was at the door now. Her hand traced the curve of violets over her ear. She saw an arm rising, separating her from the dining room.

"Staff shall enter from the kitchen," he said.

Across the jasmine sea she saw Caslin's back among the candles. She started across to him. The waiter grabbed her arm. "Ma'am!"

Eyes flickered, heads turned among silver salad forks, and wine swirled in glasses hastily set down.

[23]

"Did you bring your apron?"

"No . . ."

"Find one in the kitchen. Hurry, serving is underway." He slapped her on the thigh.

Caslin Krasavage turned— "And that dress is unsuitable." —seeing her— "But he knows me!" —rising from his chair— "And no flowers."

He pulled the violets from her hair. She turned away, seeing them crushed into a spittoon. She fled, not crying. The hallway was long. Her door loomed drunkenly. She clawed the knob, heard the latch give way as she fell in upon her bare existence. A rose-colored satchel held nothing more of her than two more worn dresses, a camisole, a pouch of corn flour to mire her tearless cheeks, and minor articles of a woman bereft of her own leaving, even as she carried her leaving about with her. She weaved on her feet, willing the tears to come. *If I can get the crying started I can take it.* Her eyes blurred, but she was not crying. *Damn! I have my right I have my right.* She gathered the folds of her best dress between clenched fingers. She tore at seams and hems, brought the cloth to her teeth, tore her sleeves from her arms, rent the bodice until her tight lifted breasts lay exposed in her heaving garment.

The door opened behind her. She saw shadows fall backward into the darkened room from the gaslights in the hallway.

"Daliah," he said.

She did not cover her exposure; turned and pulled in her tears. Her hair, without the combs' and flowers' restraint, unfurled long across her shoulders. She was dun-colored in the gaslight.

"Don't you be thinking of buying me that store-made dress," she said.

He took a step into the room. "He does not work here anymore."

"I don't need that dress," she said. He touched her hair.

"We know it would not fit you," he said.

He stood at her feet with brass-colored boots. The linen fell from her waist. She fell with it, lifting a foot in her hands to remove his boot. She did not hold it long; removed the other and he moved before her in unshod feet, treading quietly without towering. He was unkempt again. His disquiet surrounded them. His hand fumbled at the closing door. Seeing what she wanted she sat back on the bed. *I have my rights,* she cried into her hands, falling, swimming through the torrents of not weeping, sobbing and fumbling childlike at the airs between them, not between them. *Burl don't even know what Florida is. He can drink and pay taxes by himself all he wants now.* The air was heavy, congealed against sheets, soft and tight drawn, and yet contoured. Bedded; no longer wedded.

THE HOUSE SAT BACK FROM THE GATE IN A CROWN OF palmetto trees. Caslin helped her down from the carriage, holding her hand. He did not let it fall as they stood, giving her an ill-feeling of possession. She disliked him holding her hand. She did not like the familiarity. She had been married to Burley sixteen years. The house was oddly shaped. She followed the beginning soar of posts, and her eyes dropped back amazed to see no second story. A single dormer window protruded like a Federal growth on a most unsouthern roofline, high pitched and narrow.

She hurried up the wide steps, and into the wide hall, saw first the brass lamp reaching from the low ceiling, two chairs on a neglected parquet floor; the drawing room with sofa, a mahogany table and straight chairs; a dining room with huge table and ten chairs, a sideboard. Each room held fewer furnishings, fewer of her footballs as she returned to the foyer where Caslin stood hat in hand on the flawed floor.

"You are disappointed. It's never what one expects."

"Are you moving in?"

"I have lived here twelve years," he said.

She followed at his elbow. He did not ask; she followed as a matter of course as she had the days after Chattanooga. But she stopped at the threshold to this room. The bed was huge, four-poled, and flanked by side tables. The fireplace arched across one wall behind massive andirons. An octagon table barely allowed four chairs to surround it. A dusty yellow mirror on the chifforobe reflected a room crammed with rugs, books, and chesterfields.

"I live here," he said.

Lamps sat with untrimmed wicks. The fireplace was cold, dark, and ashless. Krasavage moved freely among the collection, pausing to straighten a chair, before opening drapes at a window row. He was a shadow among his shadows, moving by the windows with the agility of light. A garden was outside the glass, nothing planned or ornamental. A green twilight closed around the sash, a sea of cypress, and moss, and rhododendron radiant and cool; there seemed a constant wind. Under the trees on cropped grass were a small table and two chairs. Caslin came to her, passed her, saying, "I smell wood fire from the kitchen."

The clanking of pans spilled into the hallway. She could not enter his room without invitation. She backed across the parquet seeing at once the intended proportion, the promise of rising stucco and balustrade. The stairs drew her, formal, majestic, and handwrought; leading nowhere. Without the second floor the curve of steps rose stunted below the ceiling, leading to a single door that stood in the shadows. The railing rubbed lightly beside her hip. The door was barely five feet high, not even set squarely in the alcove at the end of the stairs. She touched the door.

"Daliah, please come down," he said.

THEY HAD A MEAL OF CHICKEN, BLACK BEANS, AND RICE; they walked in the garden gloom; they lay in bed in the April night. He held her hand again. She left it dead against his flesh as she spoke.

"How big is this place?"

"I own most of the land in a wedge between Ona and Chahula," he said. "Run three thousand head of cattle and a few hundred horses."

"Racing?"

He rose on one elbow. "You ever been to a horse race?"

"My uncle once run in East Hickman. When I was eight the family went to the fairgrounds and watched him lose to an old army mare in '67." She looked at the trophies on his mantel. "He forfeited the horse in the race. He walked home to Spears."

"I mean a real race. The Derby?"

"My Uncle Cletus lost a horse in '67. Weren't nothing but a fairground grass lot. Two horses. Ain't that a real race?" she said. "You look at me like that. I've been nowhere. I've seen nothing."

"Army horse," he said.

Daliah laid her head upon his chest. She was surprised at first that though firm, he was yet comfortable—not sinewy and carved like Burley. She was surprised, too, when she heard his heart. It beat strong and slow. She ceased to wonder why he kept no clocks. She thought, *If I can just get my heartbeat in time with this man. If I can only—* She stopped thinking when something came to her.

"I can't keep up a house this size," she said.

"I have help," he said.

"No, I mean, a woman should keep up a man's house." She raised her head again, gave up his heart for a minute to see his mouth say it.

"I'm not Burley," Caslin said. He sighted down his nose at her, laid a hand aside his nose as if he was amused.

So I've heard it, she thought. "Kiss me," she said.

"Why?"

"Because you're not Burley. Kiss me," she said again.

His mouth tasted like bourbon and cigars. She did not find it unpleasant after years of buttermilk and plug tobacco. She found his heart again and placed it below her ear. She stroked his nightshirt, and knowing Caslin could not see her face, she smiled.

He held her breast, and she smiled again.

"Was your life that hard?" he asked.

"Hard enough," she said.

"I will make it better."

She found her rhythm. It was their hearts beating. "I'll see what I can do for you sometime," she said.

[28]

A SINGLE CANDLE BURNED ON THE TABLE BY THE WINdows. The drapes were drawn again. She heard movement of tupelo in the constant breeze, and there were noises like her Kentucky, but deeper, of a greater volume than in the gloom of the trees. She was straight awake on her back staring into the flickers of the candles. The furnishings stood taller in their shadows; the four poles of the bed danced and made eight on the wall over her head. She rose and saw her head drift among the bedded spires. She lay back, thinking, *It ain't like being dead. I'll wash a dress tomorrow, and my stockings. Three thousand head of cattle. Two hundred horses. Poor Uncle Cletus. Just an old army mare. Cass must win many races. Acres and acres with two hundred horses and this house sitting as he pleases, and empty rooms. Less to dust. The Cuban'll do that. I won't ever dust again. Maybe with rugs and some pictures—a big braided rug in front of the fireplace, and a portrait picture of Caslin with his boots and a horse or two running, and china in the dining room cabinet, and upstairs, we'll . . .*

She sat up again. She looked over at him. His forearm lay across his eyes, his mouth parted slightly and his lips dried before his sharp respiration.

She swung her legs over the side of the linen expecting the dry rustle like Burley's bed. The bedding was silent, and she moved quickly to the table and its candle. The double doors were silent on their hinges but betrayed her by letting her parquet footfalls echo back into the room before she could close them. The parquet was cold. The parlor doors were open. The room was larger than she remembered. The ceiling was high. The candlelight did not reach the carved paintless

[29]

trim. She turned in the sphere of light before the fireplace, the maw of the hearth that had known no fire. She saw the rugless expanse flow distant and sea-like from her step before the grating. "It's big enough for dancing," she said. A band played in her head, and she danced clumsily around the candle, a twirl, a bow, a return. She was not a dancer. She had no experience save the barn dances and one school party when in pigtails and gingham she waited unhesitantly across a cleared floor opposite a shy line of boys more intent on jackknives and blue marbles. She stopped. The music was replaced with dizziness and the smell of unregenerate memory. She could not dance. The room was not so large. She had it filled.

The stairs did not creak. In twelve years they had been seldom used. She did not touch the banister this time. She walked in the very center of the stairs, edging, wary and catlike, up the stairs. *I am not hurrying*, she breathed, but no clock was in the hall to time her. The door was closer, painted pale blue, uneven, and marred by paint runs. She touched it. *Daliah, please come down*, she imagined. The handle was painted blue too, cold and brassless.

The dust flowed when the door opened upon it. Her candle flickered, giving a filmy cotton candy exposure to the cobwebs, a lace texture to the dust of a feminine room. She turned quickly to close the door, and jumped at someone standing behind it. It was a dress form—draped still in brocade, sagging and featureless except where pins made a dart and the material had given way to gravity. The dress had no color, across from the window it was sun faded and lifeless. Piled at its side were many hatboxes. She opened one, traced the cool satin ribbons, blue and long flowing down her back when she placed it on her head. It matched the dress, was intended to complete a perfect harmony. It was now a song off-key, a quiet sad music. A music box serenaded her with a tinny French melody; the tune dissolved in the bleak air over personal stationery once perfumed and long absent of scent (unless some smallness of verbena yet lingered in the dust) ; unmonogrammed linen handkerchiefs that might have caught at the corner of a mouth, patted small lips, and then been placed away in a beaded bag; favorite female books, their pages filled with dance cards, colorless pressed roses from corsages, or letters with masculine lettering and faint girlish pennings and elder faded scratches from spidery hands or parishioner relatives long dead and less than keepsake. A few well-made furnitures stood attention among the boxes; among them a cedar wardrobe, its wood grain like colored faience flowing like clear water over reflective pebbles. She stroked its doors, and opening them, was overpowered by the odor. Handsewn quilts lay under nettings and lace cloths. Candy tins of letters released words like ice melting into the spring of her ears. She burrowed into another woman's memories. She touched them, yet with no memory going into them, she was able to see the glaring error in the museum. It was abandoned. Without patrons for the exhibition, the caring passed without notice. The curator—she breathed his name—Caslin Krasavage.

She blew out the candle. She had never been afraid of the dark. And with the silence Daliah grew calm. She saw nothing yet. The lighter outline of the doorway opened into the vacant low ceiling of the foyer, and as the light faded, the blue of the window came like the lighting of another candle. She sat at the window. The lawn to the gateposts paled between black-crowned palmettos. *Believing's not so hard. Might not even be real silk. And no cake from store-bought tins ever tasted better than my banana spice.*

Trees ended at the gate, and beyond the road the dry grassland of the ranch began, stretching to the far distant Peace River.

She burrowed into the quilt from the wardrobe, sat again at the window. Seeing the grave of tupelo surrounding the misshapen house afloat in a sea of grass, she sighed, and gave in and found the hollow among her needs. *What is he to be needing from me?*

––––––––––

The sun was on her face, and turning over on an imagined soft bed, she found abrupt emptiness like falling, seeing him through the haze of her lashes. He stared into her eyes. She woke fully, startled, and drew the quilt over her chin.

He moved to the window. It was the only light, and the air was grainy. In the sun the treasures she had discovered were dirty, less valuable.

"What am I going to have to tell you?" he said.

She looked at him. "I didn't ask you a thing."

"I know you don't sleepwalk."

She did not flinch, did not let on she was ashamed.

"I wanted to ease you the asking. You are impatient that way, Daliah."

"I can't say I'm sorry."

"I was going to see the ranch hands put up new fences. I thought you might try the door while I left you here. Maybe it would be the heat to tire you. You decide very fast."

"Burley took me sixteen years."

He took a seat on a trunk opposite her and the window. The sun was on him now, and she saw his youth again. His hair was uncombed, his shirt unbuttoned, and he wore slippers; yet he smiled, and took her hands, again.

"She was my wife."

"And?"

"What is it you think you must know—or better, what do you think I can tell you? That she is dead, been dead these twelve years? Dead as long as this half a house has stood."

He fumbled with the trunk's lock, a lock a decade unused, to pull out a sheaf of architectural drawings in a tight roll.

"Oh, I saw you looking at the house when we drove up. It is a monstrosity. Was not meant to be. See . . ." He unrolled the sheets. He turned them for her. He saw that she did not understand, and finally pointed to a page of fading blue lines.

"Where?" she said. "There's nothing here."

He stopped. "I couldn't see finishing it. We had the stairs in. I was standing here at the top. There was no roof, nor walls, nor nothing standing here. The wind was right up among the palmettos. Me, thirty-five steps up in the wind looking for miles over grassland, and Pinin called up to me she was dead." He rolled the plans back together, rolled away his dream. "I can't recall coming down. I know every one of those thirty-five fool steps up to here. I count them up; I count them down. My gut strains every time I have to come up here."

"Did I hurt you—making you come up?"

He seemed not to hear. "I had the builders roof her over, put this single dormer to give me a single space to stand straight in out from under the rafters." He turned and asked, "How much do you think I hurt?"

"You don't play fair. I don't think you would have

left knowing I was on my way up. I was here every minute since you called me down. You don't hurt much at all. Why, you don't even have the door locked!"

"I have few visitors."

"Then it ain't a museum sideshow! It's one of them mausoleum things," she said. "Shoot, you don't hurt at all."

"You are hard!" He fastened the lid once more on the trunk, locking the contents away from ridicule. He stood in the window-way; she saw the fine unshaven face above her, the flaring of his nostrils as he breathed. "Did Burley make you that way, make you caustic . . ."

"You had ten years!"

". . . make you rude. Why did you leave him?"

"I had eight children out'n that man. I owe him nothing."

"The children?"

"Mattie's fifteen. She'll take on the house and the other kids. She's done most watching of the older ones while I was busy with Carlene, Brett—I mean Burgess."

"Brett?"

She breathed harder, in time with his respiration. "Carlene's twin. He's dead. Five years."

"So you know. I grant you feel half what I do with my ten years. I may have had twice as long to forget, twice as long to dwell."

His hands were clenched in his pockets. She saw the knuckles straining the fabric like a boy with a fistful of marbles—like Burgess.

And she had come no distance at all, to stand among forgotten silks and spring morning sun shining on a man's face which strained in her memory barely six days. She was confronted again by marble fists that strained only a better grade of cloth.

"You saying you love me?" she said.

[34]

His hands went slack, and all the marbles fell in one best shooting, clacking in all directions, leaving two marbles—she, the one he had aimed upon and missed; so it was her turn.

"I just don't want to need anymore. You do that for me?" She rose beside him in the window. There was no room between the boarding and the many-paned glass. She pressed against him, speaking into his face, his face that was flawless and morning lit.

"I can't be knowing what you want from me. Do I have to go to the races with you just to erase the shame I haven't remembered good enough about East Hickman and not this Derby place? Do I have to let you buy me silk dresses?" Her words clacked. "Do I have to love you?"

She thought he would turn and look down over her. She felt his breath against her cheek, could see his hands flexing in his pockets. The tendons of his throat tightened, he swallowed, then spoke dry. "I have touched you. I need to touch you, to have you stand with me in windows and ask if you have to love me." He would not look at her. His eyes searched space only inches from his sight. He left the playing circle, gave her the game. "I will show you. Never say you love me." And he kissed her, and with the same intimate movement was gone from the attic, leaving her with a question. Looking down over the stairs after him, her hand caressed the faded cloth on the dress dummy, and the dummy air rang with the imaginary clattering of marbles falling into her winner's drawstring bag.

DAYS WERE SIMPLE AND SHE THOUGHT SHE LIKED THEM so. He showed her the ranch, and once, stepping down from the carriage into a herd of steers, with Caslin striding a hundred yards away to speak with a foreman, a bull ran toward her. Caslin yelled, yelled frightened for her to run, to get into the carriage, but she reached down for a strong branch and whumped the bull hard across the forehead, yelling, "Gwon." She dropped the stick as the steer loped complaining away into the herd, and with Caslin remonstrating at her side, she wiped the black filth of tupelo on the skirt of one of the old dresses she wore around the ranch, saying, "Shoot, was just a fool cow." They boated on the Peace River, dipping oars into a flurry of dragonflies. In late May they traveled to the seashore, and there on the Gulf, Daliah stood long among the tangle of driftwood, mangrove roots, and white sand and prayed thanks to God for letting her know the sea. Caslin ran far away on the tidal sand. His trail of steps filled with brackish water. The ruinous sun turned the footprints silver in the white sand, and gray water took them, leaving Caslin far away upon a hillock, looking back at her, then growing nearer as he splashed through the incoming sea to take her higher on the beach. She breathed harder, her head dizzy as the sun stole away, and Caslin gave her the sea. In June they were at home, Caslin chewed a pencil over a roll of drawings at the desk. She sat across the room doing little, watching him, and with her hands spread wide across her stomach, knew it was not the time to tell him.

"We must be in Tampa. Mr. Plant will expect me at the new hotel. Are you up to it?"

"Hotel roomers don't bother me. It's people what runs them I have the problem with. Can you get them all fired?"

"All two hundred of them."

She would try him at his word; at her need. "I can't

[36]

be going with what I got. I've ruined one dress already
. . . and we know where the best of them got me."

"We'll have to buy you more dresses, and shoes and
. . . underthings, I imagine." He sat opposite her over a
low table. From that distance she could not tell the
color of his eyes in his almost featureless brow. His eyes
were water blue, with the texture of china. Across the
room, his words were just as pale and colorless; he said,
"Buy what you need. What you'll have."

"What about the other shame?" she said. She
pushed further back in her chair, watching him.

"I can explain you."

"In the same bed?"

He sat forward, his elbows on his knees, his long-
fingered hands over the table. He watched his hands;
she saw his hands turn over, then turn back; returned
them both to cover his knees, as if to say to her loudly,
"Why bother."

"I'm going to bed," he said.

She listened to him remove his clothing behind
her: the careless drop of his boot, the silent rush of fine
shirt linen draped over a chair, and the cold sheet of
the bedclothes turning down. She kept her eyes on the
great lamp before the drawn drapes, saw the sudden half
dimming as he lowered the bedside lamp, which made
the furniture at her side of the room loom frighteningly
toward her as they rushed from the light of the remaining lamp. With its extinguishing she moved into bed
beside him, thinking, *Tampa better be what he wants to
test. It ain't going to be me. I'm going to like it, going
to make liking Tampa easy.* The sheets were cold. Caslin lay far to his side of the bed. She inched to the
middle, composed her body and the bedding as if she
was the only one laying in the dark, the only one carefully floating in the familiar sleepy cocoon.

THIS BED WAS LARGER. SHE AWOKE IN THE EARLY TAMPA morning. Yesterday was a muddle, decisions fell left and right among her overworked thinking, remembering the mass of the Tampa Bay Hotel rising out of its sprawl beside the Hillsborough, the canna and hibiscus roadway where rickshaws carried peerage noiselessly as she stood at the steps of a thousand-foot veranda. She looked upward at the twelve bulbous domes on the roof floating above the trees. An orchestra played Strauss from a shell on the grass as she moved across the porch into the shadow of horseshoe arches and manicured ferns and moss flowers. Inside the Alhambra Hotel, Moorish pendants draped over European crystal and period pieces. Mr. Plant gave welcome and kissed her hand. She said little more than hello in her rehearsed afternoon voice, paid slight attention to the arrangements, and was mute to the swell as evening came into dinnertime, even said little at the table except for an aside to Caslin: "There's not nothing on this menu looks like what I would even think about cooking." After the meal, they sat again on the veranda on white straw furniture and the shadow of an arch cut wide across Caslin's chest, putting the sun across his broadcloth, and left his shoulders and face in blackness.

"Fireworks. Looks best out on the river."

"You mean them boats?" she said. "The sun's near out. You want to go out in the dark?" Her eyes strained to see the welts that were boats upon the river. The reflection of the sun lay against the docking, and the scatter of boats converged, moving to shore like iron filings to a magnet.

She hiked her skirt above her small ankles, lifting the green taffeta as she stepped into the boat, moving

[38]

side to side as the craft turned circles once, twice, before the boatman withdrew from the throng at the dock, and now antimagnetic sculled onto the river. She lost ground, for an instant became indecisive, reached out for a word with Caslin to take the boat back in, but seeing others flee the bank, she settled back and breathed. *Maybe I'll just let him see me being sick.*

"You better listen," she said.

A rocket climbed the sky and rained over them. Her head pounded. A pinwheel drew him into its embrace, lighted him as he turned, feeling her grip at his arm.

"Damn you, I'm pregnant," she said.

———

THE ROOM WAS SO LARGE, STARING AS SHE WAS INTO THE ceiling, she saw no corners, walls, or ceiling meeting partitions, just an open whiteness of new paint, and the soft summer drowse of morning sun flooding through the open balcony. She breathed crape myrtle. She heard music and lawn bowling below. *I can't think. April May June . . . ten eleven weeks. My God, it could be his . . .*

Caslin sat inside the door, smiling. He had flowers.

"Forgive," he said.

"For this whole week," she said.

"You were afraid of my reputation for bedding you in public." He gave her white stephanotis, pale and starlike. He sat with her on the bed, fondling her fragile hand.

"I'm already married."

"It can be set aside . . ."—And watching in his eyes, she mirrored her questioning—"so quietly," he said.

Maybe because he had breached it, had said marriage, which was as far, as legal she imagined he could arrange for them, she passed it by, set it aside.

[39]

"I just said I was pregnant, that's all," she said.

"Haven't you decided yet? What have you to go back for? What can that Kentucky farmer give you I can't give a hundred of?"

"You forget. I'm the one who thinks you're a millionaire. Don't offer me money to have a baby. I'm not a—" She faltered.

"Harlot," he said.

"Harlot," she said.

"Do you know what you say?"

"These people have not seen me enough for you to let them judge. Take me down," she said, rising out of their bed. She crossed to the bureau, letting him see her nakedness in the sunlight as she dressed. She was white skinned, firm, not pretty, however, more handsome than beautiful. She powdered her face whiter with corn flour. "Let them see me, talk with me. Ask me anything. What do you know about their thinking? You're blind, been blind twelve years since that woman died. What would a woman of Mr. Krasavage say to them what promenades around in white gloves in a June as hot as this?"

"Do you know what you are doing?" he said.

"Look," she said, pulling a box from her rose satchel. "I'm even going to wear these ear bobs your money bought me. Right in the middle of the day."

She smiled between the flash of gaudy earrings as they descended the grand stairs. She gripped his arm when another lady neared, and on the lawn she made them walk the promenade, steered them away from the river, and in front of the orchestra shell drew Caslin over to the lawn, looking out over the cannas where the game was being played.

"What is this they're doing?"

He explained croquet to her, taking her aside a few minutes, handing her her own shallow mallet and painted wooden ball which she fisted, unmoving, not feeling the texture of painted wood in her small hand, but breathing the rules and boundaries of wickets and stakes into her inexperienced thinking. Having as much as she thought she needed, she headed into the throng, the throes of the game: the swirl of matched silks, parasols in June, and other women laughing with the colored balls in their hands, while the shorter men leaned expertly on their mallets, the taller men swinging instruments at their thighs or tapping the ends into open palms. Daliah moved to her start, and straightaway sent her ball above the wickets into the center of the playing lawn. She played precisely (she was accurate at washers with her children) and though other women tittered childishly over their awkward swings, touched gloved hands to the lapels of their partners when they excused their play, Daliah did not once make vouchsafe for her mistakes. Even when Caslin gave her a pointer how to stroke smoothly with the side of her mallet, she said, "I'm not driving railroad spikes."

She clipped the ball of the man playing in front of her, and Caslin showed her about sending-away. He placed his foot on her ball and tapped the gentleman's a few feet away, both men nodding to show how deferential they could be to a woman's game. She said, "Can't you hit it farther than that?" She aimed for another player's ball, moving methodically, hitting, sending away, hitting, sending away, not even trying for the wickets. Other players talked hushed when she struck, making pained faces, shocked as she powered each and every one away, sending some balls from the court into the cannas, and one even passing through and rattling down the promenade with its owner running after it among the turned heads of strollers discovering the play. Caslin touched her arm once; she swung away, again keeping her eyes on the mallet and the follow-through and not looking up at his pinched face, saying, "You're messing my swing." He moved to the sidelines as she stroked again. Players placed their mallets and balls in the racks, and retreated from the field; others hunted their balls among the flower beds, until Caslin and Daliah were alone in the center of the lawn. She struck Caslin's ball, whooped, and finally looking up at him and seeing the empty field and the scatter of mallets, placed her ball next to his to send it away, stopped, picked up his bright green ball, and heaved it as far as she could, letting it ride far up arching down as she stepped over the cannas, pulling the bobs from her ears.

SHE COULD SEE THE DOOR HE WOULD HAVE TO COME through, the very threshold of summer air, overscented with cut flowers. She laid siege to the mirror, attaching her eyes to the spot behind her where she knew he would appear. *It was the ear bobs. They weren't big enough for them to see swinging in the sun.* Up from the bench and into the window which again was a mirror on a world she did not understand, a mirror without substance because it was reversed from all her experience, she threw the jewelry into the calm surface to shatter its glass reflection, and was surprised to see the earrings sail through without breaking the June morning haze.

"You can't tell me I didn't win that game," she said.

"They'll give you first prize," he said, exactly in the mirror where she knew he would be, motionless, dull about the margins even as the mirror flattened his height in its amber dustless light.

[42]

"But I've done had eight children!" she said (and was wrong. She had only seven, the son had fallen from her mothered walls, resting quickly in her backyard cemetery and in the twin Carlene's exact eyes. She had no bottom for trying after Brett). "You want I should deliver this child into your hands?" She would not will the tears, although they found her cheeks, barren and floured.

"I'll give you what you need. I promise you that. Whatever you need."

She lied. *It will not be his. Let Burley dare to claim it* and wished she had not thrown the earrings so far.

"I said anything," he said.

"Go downstairs and see if there ain't a trophy of some kind for them wicket games."

HER FINGERS SETTLED INTO SEWING. CASLIN WAS IN ONA picking up the mail, sending wires of accounts. Over her head the dull hammering ceased and after a silence, a single board fell by the window, tearing down through the palmetto into a pile of shingles and rafters. The white table and the two chairs had been moved from the once quiet green, and now leaned unprotected and covered with dust beside an outbuilding. There was a rug on the floor bordered in green and spring flowers, a sofa near the parlor fireplace where she sat, and a new clock on its mantel ticking below the frame hung without portrait above. Caslin had two more sittings. She had forgotten—he was in Ona for a sitting with the painter also. She forgot details; she placed it with her pregnancy. She dropped a stitch, pulled it loose, and, losing the pattern she was in, dropped her needles as feet came thumping down the stairs.

[43]

"Mum," the feet said.

She looked out through the parlor doors, saw a lean head bending down to see her and saying again, "Mum, what want to do with these?"

She carried her six months, treading her way by the light of the open front door through the boxes and barrels that had come down out of the attic, spread ownerless, dusty about the parquet floor; looked upward, blinded by the September sun through the open roof. Hot, pale air struck her face. The workman held the dress form, clumsy and smudged and faded in his hands. "It ripped, Mum," he said.

"Bring it down with the others. All out to the barn. So it ripped. It was ruined just being up there," she said, turning to close the jarred door of the cedar chest, and saw the wagon motionless on the dust which, close to the ground, compact and rutted, was shifting, nostril-filling and hopeless. Caslin sat in the wagon bed, a relief sculptured by a patina of dust against the Florida September sky hanging low to the Peace River. Pinin reined the carriage between the high gateposts and drew up, scattering the motionless dapple of tupelo on the drive as he backed to the front portico.

He was out of the wagon, trailing his earth over the parquet, carrying its tide over the clutter before she could celebrate him home. He wandered among the boxes, touched them, caressed them with hands and eyes.

"Well, you can't leave it up there," she said. "There's no roof, for God's sake!"—and saw him standing erect over a barrel broken open amid falling books and mold-rotten fabric in the sun of the open stairs. His hand lay tight over her removal, unapproachable, reproachable; and seeing, she said, "All right. All right then. It's just out to the barn."

[44]

She filled the barrel again, the worn books in a none too neat pile, and closed it over. "You got the wagon already up to the door, let the Cuban take this on over to the barn. All right. All right then. Take it over yourself," she said.

The dress dummy was the closest at hand. She held it boldly over her stomach, and carried it, squat-walked it through the door. He stopped her. He took the dress from the form, taking care with the pins and the never-threaded buttons, folded it carefully, the faded bosom decrescendoing onto the mustard folds of the skirt. Her eyes never left his hands, thinking rapidly and without direction at how he labored, and placed the fine garment neatly, orderly, finally into the second shelf of the cedar wardrobe recently vacated from the attic. Not believing herself, she said, "Save me them pins."

He gave the pins to her, and not removing the dust covers from the wagon, set the load on the porch, and took half an hour to load everything from the foyer onto the wagon, shifting to make a single load. She stood beside the door under the shadow of tupelo, watching, not even leaving for the half hour it took the wagon to run around the side of the house and down the yard road where she watched Caslin lift down from the bed each box, barrel, the cedar wardrobe in its turn, and carry them into the darkness of the barn. She watched Caslin walk the road under the sun; and beside her now, she heard him say, "I'm not angry. Not even a roof up there."

"Had to," she said.

"Had to," he said. "She was already down and gone out to the barn before I left this morning, wasn't she? Nothing for me to fret but the carrying out and the lifting up.

"Besides," he said. He called upward into the

[45]

blindness of falling ceiling dust. More plaster rained on him before his word brought the feet thumping down again.

They moved the covered furnishings in from the porch, taking them around her for she stood unmoving in the middle of the floor. But she came running child-like as Caslin uncovered one, bursting in upon its doors and cherry inlay, fingering the polished piece, the brass handles and drawers sliding easily under her hands. A mirror matched the credenza so she sent the workman up the stairs for a hammer and nail for hanging. Caslin drew her over to another covered object. It was lower built, more symmetrical; she cringed when Caslin pulled back the canvas. The cradle was of cherry also, richly carved, posts above smooth veneers.

"It's a sturdy one," he said. He did not notice she shrank from it, reaching for the arm of the chair behind her. He traced the headboard, tipped the balance, and the cradle flowed between where he knelt on the floor, his hand on his chin on the end support. "My mother had sons, all Krasavages like my father, tall, quiet, carrying men. I heard her telling of her father, Haberstraum Fox, and her grandfather, Otho Fox." He stopped the rocking, looking over at her as she gripped the chair white-knuckled. He rocked again, chin in hand. "A man needs an heir, to amass something just to pass it on, even if it's only the color of his hair." He caught her eyes. "I'm sorry you don't have a gut for this child, that you won't grieve the years for him. But he's mine."

She shifted in the chair.

"He's Otho Haberstraum Fox Krasavage," he said. He took to rocking the cradle slowly back and forth . . .

. . . and with the baby bedded he tipped it gently. The child was male and covered lightly even though it was December, and rained.

Daliah had not seen the baby. She was not spent, though the headboard showed her handprints where she had fisted the birthing, carrying the soft wood under her nails as she strained his passage, and a midwife-nurse and a doctor had burrowed into the thick cloudiness of her pain, and piles of white linens towered and swam in the crying of her unseen child as the doctor lifted it from her, and she, looking away and turning over on her side as she had not been able since the time of the September dust, gave into the slackness and slept.

Dreaming was a song she remembered, beginning lazily like her pregnancy but then swelling in counter-melody and discord as the string of notes became scales spiraling upward, her actions against Caslin's actions: the October morning when Caslin placed his portrait in its frame and it was as she had planned, the boots and horses running accurate if not expertly on the canvas with flat brushstrokes, and even his eyes were captured waterless, translucent and blue. He brought home furnishings, long tables, sofas which he placed as he wished. Little was what she wanted (she was fearful of her tastes and said nothing) — everything long and spaced, creating aisles with furniture, rectangular frames, runners in the hallways dark and muddy. She wanted tall chairs, clocks and knickknackery, straight lamps—something to break his proportion. The stairs now moved upward into a sweep of fanlight windows, where the sun rose, came full, and failed. She would stand early in the morning and watch the workmen come across the long eastern drive, watch as the dark Spanish and southern heads disappeared when they passed under the portico to take task in some rearward room; in the evening she watched with the fading red sun on her face swallowing the newness of stucco paint as the workmen receded. The men were plastered and painted and sweaty—a silence of

[47]

exasperated breath, the slip of one final note as the door suffered them pass, for she did not go to see out the eastern window. Caslin somehow had come up to find her standing red and fired in the hallway light.

"I had the table and chairs cleaned. They can go back under the trees," he said. In the stairwell he, too, was red, and wearing brown as was his habit around the ranch, he all but disappeared in the downward rush of the mottled steps.

"I don't want the chairs under the trees," she said. She glared down over the railing at him. "Leave them where they are. Let them rot. I hate that lie too."

"Dali," he said. She moved past him, taking one step at a time, saw that he was carrying the cradle up to the nearly finished nursery, moved hastily despite her pregnancy and crossed the still barren floor. The parquet had been taken up, scraped clean and left in piles.

For a moment she sank to her knees and placed pieces back on the floor, thinking, *Never my way. Can't furnish, floor, or have a baby on my own.* She was out of order, was without pattern. She turned over the piles that were at hand. She surrendered and threw a handful of the tiles out the open door the workmen had not bothered to close in their sunset running, threw them into the dying red as she aimed for the gatepost, and trailing behind her, dropped many, still threw until she stood in the low curry color of the roadway and cursed as she threw the parquet back at his house. She gave up, her hands were empty, clenching, opening, and cursed that she had no more to throw. *Damn I've got to have peace. I can't lie to me too. He knows. He can't help but know.* She was in the county road and because it was not his she breathed easier a moment, free of him, free of what could not be hers because she had lied; and the symphony of wind blew up its trumpeting among the top leaves and under the completed eaves of the house. He stood in the door. She clenched her fist and with the coming of blood, breathless, pained, she fell to the earth, soundless except for the decrescendo of the palmetto rustle and the dreamlike shuffling of his feet on the drive.

She turned over once more, coming out of the haze knowing relief, and dreamless. The room was washed green in the rain, the wet tupelo brushing and twinkling in the December wind. In front of her eyes was a mound of white laying close, drowning also and washing in the green. And expectantly movement came from it, a puffing of the coverlet as the red of a small fist pried out of the folds. She watched it rise again, and fall, a flicker before she reached out and took the hand in hers. The blood beat faint, warm, and bird-fast between her fingers. She smoothed back the edge of the blanket and saw the red face and the almost lidless eyes, and the soundless breath bubbled between pursed lips. She lifted the baby close, saw the movement of its hands, saw the grateful relaxing into fists as she brought him to her breast. She smiled at the remembered suckling.

After three years, oddly it was the same, more like the first, scared, surprised, thinking herself incapable. Yet she had sustained for fifteen years, from Mattie through four strong nursing sons. Then there had been the twins when more than once she had nursed Carlene and Brett one after the other while one (usually Carlene—she was stronger, and Daliah guessed she favored Brett) wailed with fists thrown out as the other drew, filled, was laid back in the center of the bed, and the other came to her already pursing before reaching her breast. She would sit in the finished gloom, quiet herself as if her final milk had drained, and the sunless afternoon or early morning darkness drew about her while she wept. When Brett had failed it had been morning. She had gone to raise them wailing from the crib and found a single voice instead of a chorus. She absently brought him to nurse, sitting back in her chair by the bed. It was minutes before she knew he was dead, so she sat deafened to Carlene's bellowing with the wild waving hands, and cradled Brett, now without the weight of life that on any previous morning was just routine. She ran through the breezeway from the house into the hard-packed yard bordered in broken bricks and mimosa trees, running along the forever muslin fences clutching Brett to her chest. The cemetery of family stones was on her left. The August pear tree's rotten fruit hummed with wasps. Burley came down from the mule shed, hame in hand, and harness broken. He said. "What about Carlene?"

At the kitchen tub she scrubbed the emptiness where Burley had taken Brett from her arms. She lathered up to her elbows, rinsed, lathered again, setting up a splashing against Carlene's screaming from the bed— screaming until her red face held the volume no longer and lapsed and struggled. Daliah stood over her; held her on her lap at the funeral as the dirt rattled on the pine coffin. She actually had to wash the dirt from her hands for she threw one gathered hand of yellow clay into the hole, saw it fall slowly, carrying a trickle over the wood, which she did not see for she had walked away with Carlene at her breast.

This child was no different. The same small weight, length, sprawl of nursing . . . like all her others. Like Brett too. Then she remembered to look. She forced the boy's head back. The lips still pursed, but finding air, stopped, and the eyes came open. They could be green. The baby started to cry. She returned him. They could be green.

She began writing the letter with her free hand, canting the paper to write the greeting into the soft coverlet; found she could not, and set the paper aside. She was not clear in her thinking anyway, could not join into words. So she put thinking aside, letting the words fail under her hands. Besides, it was December, and Christmas could not be a time for deciding. She joyed in Caslin's gifts: a dress to celebrate the return of her small figure, a handwrought mirror which carried her reflection in amberless light, and a diamond. She had seen so few diamonds, and never one up close. She carried it to windows and let the December light catch, play. And it was January, and the child was small; and February came distant like the threat of northern wind, rain, and the earth was brown-wet, and the sound of moaning cattle came to her through the curtained windows.

She sealed the envelope with wax. The soft red paraffin was formless—the wax and stationery were a Christmas gift too. She turned the letter over for a final, certain look at the address written in her great primer-formed letters, knowing the weight inside was of many similar primer-fast pages spilling over into a tale. She was relieved because the words were wrapped in paraffin and block, postmarked and gone. Caslin had carried the letter himself; she saw him put it in his tweed pocket, and she did not fear he would not mail it, that he would even read the address between the placing in his pocket and the post office in Ona.

Caslin had come in on her holding her son on her lap. They were sitting in the now uncluttered room where they had bedded, which was now his study. She still preferred the room. It was quiet, greening now in the March light. She had been wrong. He had read the address, had seen the woman's name, and must have known something akin to dread. He stood under his portrait (he had moved it himself; she had come down one morning and found a mirror in its place in the parlor; asking him, he had said, "He's like me. He needs this room too"). But Caslin was ill-composed, unlike the man in the painting, leaning at the mantel overwhelmed by the great andirons and ashes. He kicked the brick step at the hearth and said, "I mailed your letter."

She would have to tell, though Tampa Bay and the boat still swirled in her memory, and the momentary illusion of loving him was just backward in the mirror, the coming to truth was about her again. She watched him quickly, letting him in turn stand, waiting on her, and numbly reconciled to her chances, she drew the lap blanket over the child's head to protect him as she told Caslin. "I figure, if it was just a matter of days this child might have been fathered by John Burley Mead."

He laughed. "We are a marvelous thing, Daliah. You will ruin it. You have already."

She shifted in her lamp-lit brightness. The child stirred, then replaced his fists beside his head. "I have named him Otho for you," she said.

"That's just his name." Caslin rose larger before the dead fireplace, his hands white and clean, cleaving the air about him like plow tines, frustrated, awkward, without character. "This triangle is not you and me and John Burley Mead. It's between you and me—and love. You are a stranger to my love, Daliah, you know you are."

"I don't know what it is," she confessed. "Love is a funny thing."

"You think that he—"

"It's not Burley," she said.

"I'm thinking of the child."

[52]

"You want me to tell you he is when he may not?"

"Does it matter if he's Burley Mead's bastard baby or my bastard baby?" Caslin leaned away from the mantel. "Here or with him, the boy will be a doubt to you."

"Otho is my baby," she snapped. "The only doubting is from the arrogant seed of you and Burl!"

Caslin's head turned high and pained. For a second Daliah saw how he must have posed for the portrait. The lines of his jaw were taut and colored much as the painter had laid them upon the canvas. She wondered if Caslin matched the same struggle to capture his portrait as he now had to struggle with her disappointment.

"I thought it was over, the waiting, the hope, the held breath. When you came I finished building the house," he said. "I put the large windows in the upstairs hallway the way *she* wanted them. I have been suspended twelve years hoping to have her back."

"You did it for her," Daliah said flatly.

Caslin turned from his portrait. "No. I did it for myself."

"Then there's four folk here tangled in this loving."

Caslin drew taut again. "She gave me no children."

She made movements, falling over words even before she said them. "I said I was no harlot. I curse you."

He looked down from his perch, secure in his final wordings. She heard them coming, could have mouthed them with him, and did so under her breath.

"There is only one inclusive curse, all powerful, past, present, and future curse," he said. "And on your family."

The pantomime fell under her breath, falling into the face of the child she, Caslin, and John Burley damned, and now caught up in their curse.

"And on your family," she said.

SHE WAS MOVING AGAIN. UNDER ONE HAND THE HASTILY set-down luggage collapsed on its soft sides, her fingers flexing tired and traveled, and in the other hand the inevitable rose-colored satchel yet rode, seldom set down, worn, and still loved like a favorite doll. She had ridden first class on leather seats, with a dining car and a small lower berth that was at least soft. Behind her the porter said, "Ma'am." She did not hear. She breathed in the Kentucky spring air. The light was only a shade less bright than Florida. "Ma'am," he said. "Here's your chil'." She looked back at the porter standing on the last step of the train, holding out to her the white cocoon of her son. She took him lightly, and held him close, checked his breathing, shallow and like water, sleeping again. "Thank you," she said. She looked around for some dissimilarity that would make the change that had come over her noticeable to anyone better than to herself. "Spring's early this year," she said.

"Had to, Ma'am," the porter said. He swung back up to the platform. "What with two feet of snow in January, winter probably just got used up and had to let go into warm. Thankee, Ma'am."

The train moved up into its chuckling storm, grew rhythmic and away. She paid little attention. It was not like changing trains at the station, where she had stood down from one train and waited for the next to board. At the station she had seen trains' smoke approach. She knew she had to get on board, so she had watched, and had tensed against the concussion as the train swept up, sucking at her, and had swept away, leaving a vacuum to pull her skirt about her legs. It had not been her train. So she waited. And the next train had come, and she cringed against the arrival, her head tilted to the side with the muscles drawn tight, eyes closed. It slowed beside her, she was lost a moment in its storm. She had climbed up, had ridden again. She was set down into Kentucky, with the baby and the rose-colored satchel.

She walked again, taking easy measured steps from tie to tie. Two bags and a child were not cumbersome to her, coming up beside the cordwood depot and into the sandy cut before she jostled to make a new balance.

Not much farther. Don't seem near as far as the going. Why, I can see clean across this field now. Like as if the world has shrunk on me since. The mule trace in this spring was littered wound, red clay rutted and straight. She came to the fallen barn. One man stood high over the sun levering a loft board over, letting it clatter easily into a pile of planking below. Men hammered, their chests already burned by the spring sun. The roof was gone. The rest followed in pried, man-made decay. She moved quickly by, did not see, did not hear the slow swing of boards falling, and the scream of crowbarred headless nails propelled her into the rutted return of the County Line Road.

And it's April again, she thought. *Burl ain't even got that section plowed neither.*

She could see the house. It was smaller to her, a paintless possum-trot and lean-to. The wire fences were bare; no muslin cleaved to the morning dew, unseamed and unblanched. She was into the gate before she saw him under the locust. She made a halting step. She shifted the baby higher above her hip. Jaretta stood in the doorway; she held Carlene's hand. There was nothing in her face. "God," Daliah said. Under the mimosa Burgess looked up from his dirt. He spoke up at her with a four-year-old's contempt, calling above the cries of chickens, "It's about time, Mama."

[55]

NOVEMBER
1963

DISON JANE WAS A PHOTOGRAPH. HER FACE CARried the flat light of a daguerreotype—brown, dark eyed, and without angular planes. When she spoke her lips remained drawn thin as though caught in the instant of a photo flash, untextured and pursed smooth as agate stones. She saved her grandchildren's photos too, tacked them about the walls, on shelves, and on the mantel in gold eight-by-ten frames. Samuel would not look at the great ears he had only recently grown into. They must have been Mead (or Brownlee) ears; they couldn't have come from the dimensionless Dison Jane Sisk.

"He talks of his mother," she said. "You notice that? Otho acquaints little to John Burley. Men hold so little blame among themselves. He goes so far to quit Dali Brownlee, I suspect he down in believes she's guilty. Why else would he defend her innocence so?"

The front porch was littered with potting soil. Dison Jane turned over the packed earth in the boxes lining the railing with a trowel. Her moss roses had bloomed there in spring. She was preparing the flower beds for winter. The beds beyond the porch, reaching up the hill toward the road, were already turned; the iris bulbs had been separated by colors; sacks of white and violet and yellow were beside the door. She had begun her final yardwork in October, taking the prunings from tea roses from the far beds bordered in brick teeth at the fence; the tiger lilies, cockscomb, and hydrangea from the hill; and the cosmos from beside the porch wall between the railing and the brick walk that circled the house. Now that it was November she did the porch boxes, retreating each week closer toward the house so when winter came she could step inside pulling the sacks of bulbs and uprooted geraniums.

Her trowel was edged in wet earth, and she pointed it at Samuel. "Now, John Burley was the pivot. I can't believe he would turn his back for Daliah Faye to run for southern havens. I can't for sure believe she could have made it there on her own unless she sold something of value. I mean gave away what . . ." She plunged the tool in a moss box. "How old are you?"

"Sixteen," he said.

"Well," she said. "Value."

"Herself," he said.

She smiled for him. "I blush less these days. Used to be I could turn the color of dame's rockets. What did you do with the peat?"

The twine was lost in her hands. Samuel helped her unravel the string and tie some of the plastic covers around stems. "See how I had to cut behind the buds. Pruned there and the blooms were as big as saucers." She straightened, watching him over the railing, bent on his knees with his young gloveless hands balanced between twine and dried seed pods.

"Yes, when I was younger!" She sighed. "When I first met your grandpa's folks they was sitting on cane chairs in front of their home in Mercer County. It was spring, far after sundown."

Dison laid her hand aside a railing post. Samuel was still on the ground on the other side. He looked up and

[60]

saw her face behind the railing slats. From her cage she said, "At first I did not see them under the dapple of the locust and mimosa grown too big and probably no longer flowering. Coming up the walk I heard her voice first, saying, 'My God, another small-boned woman coming into the family.' 'Hush,' John Burley said, 'she's a mite bigger than you were.' Otho had my arm. I was just ahead of him, he steering me forward it seems now." The grandmother's face was pressed between the slats. Samuel thought to get up and maybe she would rise too. He did not like to see her so. She went on, "Otho was afraid of them too, only nineteen and somewhat pleased with himself after making his proposal— asking me was easier. Daliah said, 'Well, you want us to look at her from out in the road?' John was a tall man, up five steps above us on the porch. His hair was not yet gray, not even around his ears because he wore no side whiskers or any hair around his temples at all. He said, 'Dali does not understand that men choose more delicate women these days.' Then I saw his hand was on her shoulder, and she flinched it off. 'Dali has always been delicate herself; I came by her by fascination alone. Fascination outweighed her faults,' he said."

"Your knees hurt," Samuel said.

"He had a way of turning aside, stepping right by Daliah." Dison Jane smiled, her teeth firm and discolored. She smelled of onions. "Burley knew it then, weren't no holds on him by that Daliah Brownlee woman. He leaned against one of the porch posts, his arms roped around it while she talked. She was saying, 'Fascination is a funny thing, bringing together disjointed people—like you and me; or him and me; or you and her.' "

Dison sat back against the sacks of iris bulbs, dry and with unbloomed—past bloomed color.

"Of course I did not understand what she meant. I did not have the story beating about me like Otho. He took it to heart, and chose Daliah as the champion. Set her white face—yes, it was what I saw from under the porch roof, her white unlined face. And I might as admit she was vainly beautiful. I may be jealous of her for that. That she had the physical face to attract interest, to have two men—no, not two, three men in her life to love her. Otho was just like Burley. I love Otho though I fault him his blindness. I chose Burley to counter Otho. I loved him too—can't you see."

"Can't you get off your knees?" Samuel said again. He wiped a hand under his nose, smelled wet earth. His hands were black. His knees ached in the flower beds. Brick borders cut his shins. His thighs cramped. If he could move her out of pain, break her spell, he would not be ashamed she had outlasted him.

I cannot hear this, he thought. *Why don't they fight their love among themselves?*

Dison Jane was quiet only a moment, enough to draw breath. Her hands were in her apron pocket even though she wore gloves.

"It does me good to work in the earth. When I'm frustrated I take my trowel and dig it out like chickweed." She turned her head slightly to the side, laying a barren cheek on her shoulder, speaking into the cotton. "But today I got me a scythe, a young sixteen-year-old scythe to tear out the tall weeds my heart gave up on. Look," she said, pointing at the walk next to them, at the concrete laid fifteen years ago from the hill to the porch. "I did not make those fossils there."

The footprints of a child had been pressed into the concrete, flanked by a large monogram in red paint: OM.

"You will not swear those are your prints, as Otho

would not claim it was his hand which pressed them there and wrote those initials. Men do not claim sentimental things." She was struggling. "You are his namesake. You are a male baby and therefore disposed to think like him, and accept his misguidance even if he calls it love." She was almost crying.

"I have nothing, no claims on you but some little blood, and if you both are bastard babies because Otho may be illegitimate I will have some say as a mother because I know my line sure. We are good women. So I admit I dislike Daliah Faye Brownlee because she is a weakness in the line . . . a purveyor . . . a harlot. She has made Otho believe himself less pure—tainted and superstitious." She wiped her eyes with her apron. "I love him, I do, and I hate to see him pass into seventy-one years waiting to die just to prove Daliah Brownlee a better woman than I. And worse to have him make you believe the same."

"You've warned me," he said.

She reached through the rails and touched his face. The glove was coarse. He turned and kissed it.

"You are so like John Burley," she said. "He was a good farmer. Reap of us what he would: some honesty, not much fool kindness, and a little prideful love."

CHAPTER FOUR

APRIL

1892

JOHN BURLEY TURNED OUT OF SLEEP. HE DID NOT wake with a false cock crow; there was no rooster to crow. The last rooster, an aged feather-bereft bird, had met their Sunday table some weeks back with a wringing of the bird's neck, a quick snap, and a sparse spray of feathers. He turned over again, thinking maybe it was time to get another bird if only to ignore its false morning cry. The bed was empty beside him. Even with his hands thrown out over the quiet muslin expanse, he did not think it odd. She was already up. He waited to hear the clatter from the kitchen, some turning over of kindling into the cookstove, some cold iron clanking as she put the stove lids back over the tinder.

He remembered her the same through their sixteen years, unchanged. The quiet, almost gaunt woman-child walking the County Line Road. He stood beside the stretched wire fence cutting into his lunch of a cold sweet potato, black and round. His knife blade lifted the yam to his mouth, unseen because his eyes had not left the girl. That was his first. The second time he saw her the church steps had been empty and barren in autumn during a Saturday afternoon choir practice. He had left his sister at the church, and returning for her at four o'clock, walked those same steps upward into the hypocrisy (he was not a churchgoer yet) and heard the singer. He heard the singular voice, high among the "Shall We Gather at the River" chords, and he knew the voice was hers. And the next day he came to sit on a rearward pew and suffered through the sermon, though he did not hear it, did not drowse under the damnation preaching, but sat straight awake, and waited for the singing again, with the hymnal unopened in his large hands. He heard her voice, heard the same tones toll under the steeple bell as he searched her face out among the buggies and tethered horses in the churchyard. She walked with his sister and another high-waisted girl. He came up behind them and, laying a hand surprisingly on his sister's shoulder, spoke easily (he was that afraid) about Sunday dinner and how his mother would not mind another at the supper table.

Daliah demurred, saying she could not—being the only female in the family, she had to set supper for her father at home. Somehow walking beside her down the County Line Road he could not believe he had actually invited himself to dinner at her table.

It was a September afternoon, and the shadows were long. She led him through the trees to a house set alone, dark and shaded. He stepped onto the porch. He saw the veranda sag at one end. She was in the doorway, a shadow too. He followed her into the gloom, taking care to step around the barren table as she excused herself and disappeared into a back room.

He could not see and it did not matter; there was a lone chair, a table, four bench stools seasoned and repaired with hemp rope, a scarred sideboard, and a motionless rocker in front of the fireplace.

She returned, a brown dress in a brown room. She took cracked china from a shelf over the sink basin, and two well-scoured tin plates. She set the table with greens, kale and poke, flat biscuits, and a crock of buttermilk. He looked at her.

"I'm sorry," she said. "Mama died, and then Daddy, he tries."

Sitting down, he put away her apologies. He spooned pot liquor and greens into his mouth, tasted their acrid movement down his throat. She sat opposite him, not eating. She turned a biscuit over in her hands, and waiting until he was through (or at least until his spoon no longer carried the kale and poke to his lips) gave out her surprise—a singular jar of sorghum cane which she spooned over the biscuit like a dessert. She was small; fifteen, he thought. Watching her, he lost her face in her dark hair, close-laid gray eyes, and the lightless cabin afternoon.

"Why did you turn down my invite for Sunday dinner when you knowed your father wasn't going to sit down to these greens?"

She licked a finger, then set the unfinished biscuit on her plate. She pushed the sorghum closer to him and said, "Don't you want no sweets for after them greens?"

"He drinks."

She stood behind her chair and took up the sorghum crock between her hands. "He is a Brownlee. A Brownlee is no drunk," she said. She put the crock back on the shelf. He was not surprised he had not seen it before. Next to the cans and stoneware the great black-barreled pistol hung near the ceiling. She moved it aside to replace the crock.

"It's not a shooting offense."

"That pistol were the one Daddy carried in his war, out of Cairo and Paducah he carried it, and fired it as it was loaded." She lifted it. It was heavy, and uncleaned. "I've never shot a gun." She held the piece flat on her open palms. "It was a pride. Daddy lays his pride on the shelf with the can goods and the flour. How much pride does it take to mouth against a girl because she is poor?"

"I'm sorry," he said, and made to leave.

She turned the gun aside. "There's a bucket by the fence, and a spring a little farther. You ate from my plates. I could stand the water in return."

The path was behind heavy maples. The water was black. Down on his knees he was unnerved by a movement in the flood. A swarm of tadpoles bunched on the surface. He pushed them aside, feeling in the scattered darkness the damp swell of the bodies and the pulse of their squirm. He lowered the bucket, lost it underwater, and hauled it out to dip the tadpoles out with cupped hands. He thought for a moment to throw some of them far up the bank to rid the water of at least that many, but thought better. He would not be drinking the water. He lowered them back into the spring.

She would not let him reenter when he came up the path. In one hand she had a tin plate (it was hers: sorghum) and in the other was the gun. She was a brown study in the door's yawn; the tin plate and gun shone metallically, the gun barrel rode down—and then she fired one shot upward into the trees. He stopped. The gun was aimed at him.

"Daddy likes it fired now and then to keep the parts free worked out," she said.

She took the bucket from him, dropped the plate in. There was one tadpole in the water. She scooped it and pitched it into the side yard dust with a small motion. The animal squirmed dry and matted. She turned back toward the doorway. But she stopped, turned back to him. "You needn't come in to see the dishes washed. I couldn't take the chance you might mouth how I boil water."

"I'm sorry," he said. He passed out of the path, around a rusting scythe and unused bale wire. He kept his eyes on her; the gun was still in her hand.

"And," she said, "I have greens most every day." It was only her head he saw for he neared the corner of the house. "I'll be having greens and side meat next Sunday meal. You hear me. Real hog meat fried in my own pan. Daddy said so."

He was already around the next corner, back on the path that led up to the house from the spring. He heard her laughing behind him. He did not turn to see if the gun was still in her hand as she stood in the front door; he knew it would be, and the bucket of spring water still in the other.

"Inviting's a funny thing!" she called after him.

IT WAS NOT A YEAR—A YEAR OF SUNDAY DINNERS WITHOUT invitation, without guns, and actually without little courting—before they were married. And John Burley, with the eighty silent acres newly bequeathed to him by a silent uncle, stood in the door of their two-roomed unpainted possum-trot house watching Daliah get down from the wagon, which was not needed to carry her dowry goods; a tow sack could have carried it all. She had a rose-colored satchel, newly bought and nearly violent in its color against her gray bosom. She clutched its slack side to her chest; and in the other hand was the gun. She handed it to him as she passed the door.

"Daddy said you could have it as the nearest wedding present he could pretend he gave you." She added, "I told him it was special to you."

He fisted the gun, turned it to see some drunken hand had at least tried to polish it clean. He looked over his shoulder at Daliah, unamused by what little she saw, standing in the middle of their two rooms. And, hoping to match her, he aimed the gun high into the yard and pulled the trigger. Snick it went, unfired. She laughed behind him. "He gave you the gun. Nothing was said about no shells."

Cheated of even that, denied his revenge, he rested the gun untouched on a similar shelf lined with tin goods, flour, and crockery.

"I can buy shells myself," he said.

She had not moved from the center of the room, staying fast to the hewn table, four chairs, and hand-milled pine boards under her feet.

She said, "It's more than what I had. Not quite what I will want."

He took her shoulder. "We have time."

She moved from under his hands. "We will be bedding over here?" She crossed the breezeway and took up her rose-colored satchel, stepping around the doorway, and over to the unmade bed. "We will bed here as man and wife tonight. Will we have . . . union"—she chose her words—"without sheets of no kind?"

"Don't be afraid," he said, misunderstanding her attitude.

"Afraid of what? Of your man thing? I'm young. But Papa was coarse. He said as much with Mama gone as what a frightened month of marriage could teach. I'm not afraid of you—yet." She laid her hand flat upon the husk bedding, the mattress threaded and over-seamed. She held her face high in the light, musing, fascinated maybe. "Papa came home enough times drunk, needing to be put to bed. I carried him. I saw his shame. I'm no son of Noah. I'm not cast into a biblical curse out of Canaan. This is nowheres near the Promised," she said, laying aside the satchel. "And the drinking never dimmed him." She sat back on the bed. "No, I'm not afraid. Besides the dark comes early enough."

———————

HE PLOWED THE FIRST ACRES OF HIS DEED LAND THE NEXT morning. The mule held true to the furrow, knew the land far better than he, and from one end of the near field, back, forth, and turning, made less than effort with him. He could afford to watch for her. She moved in the doorway with her hands close laid over her wide hips. She did not seem to watch him. Her eyes did not look focused on anything. The ground held no fascination, nor the oblong outbuildings that were in need of attention. As he plowed he moved farther from her, the sweat dimmed his vision, and now it was his feet, not the mule's, that watched unfamiliar ground. So he did not see her leave the door, nor did he see her come up across the new furrows with the pail, covered and full of food, in her small hands at noon.

He made the turn at the far end of the field, and saw her materialize out of the clay, standing small and the same color as the ground in the shadow line of the far trees. He came up behind the mule, struggling because this was the first he had seen her since he had left their bed.

"I could have hurt you," he said.

"No more than what I expected. Not as bad as what I'd heard," she said.

She left the pail and turned, setting the bucket in the shade of the trees, stepping over the bales of unstretched fence wire and unrooted posts. He took the bucket, ate the cornbread, cold meat, and buttermilk. He watched her cross the field, watched her stand unmoving in the doorway again. He plowed until sunset.

He came across the field again. The fence posts lay as he had seen them before. He turned back across the field, coming upon them, thinking, *Tomorrow I can start on the fence.* He had the fence up during the quiet time after planting when he watched the weather, and seeds were alone seeds. She still came each noon, leaving the same food pail, not even looking up at him and his sweat. Though by midsummer she moved more slowly. He watched her, heavy with child, edge around the far end of the corn now standing in the first field, walking on the other side of the fence from where he weeded. She moved even more slowly that fall before harvest when he helped her into the wagon. She rode beside him. She did not speak because the rising dust troubled her breathing.

The courthouse square was filled. Coming into town late in the afternoon because they lived on the fringe of the county, Burley found little room to leave the wagon. He helped her down, she who had sat the seat high if not proud, came down into the dust. He pointed out the boardinghouse. She clutched her rose satchel. "I said I wouldn't mind standing the line with you." She let the bag slip a little.

He looked at the sun. It was near drawn with the courthouse dome. When it was level with the clock face he would be too late.

"I'll wait there," she said finally.

But he was not thinking of her; was carried into the line, carried right up to the very window where the clerk explained the difficulty to him.

"You see, son, when your uncle, John Mead, died he didn't make no payment on the last fall's tax. What with the probate weren't nothing but the land to pass to you. No money of the fall taxes." The clerk opened the brass-bound book. Names tumbled out under the hands as he showed Burley the lineage of his crisis, the full deeded plot, the lien, death, and his bequest—unpaid fall taxes 1875. Burley looked up at him through the caged window, his pride faltering.

"What's that hold on me?" Burley asked.

"That holds a double tax bill." The clerk tabulated on unruled paper with a blunt pencil. "One sixteen forty-two, to be exact."

"I don't have it," Burley said.

The clerk put down his pencil. He closed the book. "I'm sorry," the clerk said. "The taxes are due."

Burley was not thinking of the sheriff. The afternoon was put by when he came out, walking without haste, walking with compromise and carriage down the high courthouse stile and through the canna-bordered walks. He faced the red fanlight window coming into the dark from the boardinghouse. She waited; he could not. He came off the square, coming into dusk, under the six o'clock booming of the courthouse bell and the maddened swirl of pigeons roosting above his head; came into the lighted room, right up to the smeared wood bar, a bourbon at the counter and vomit under his feet.

The light was greasy and the faces were yellow and pale like blended whiskies in unwashed glasses. *Ain't right I got to stand the loss because an old fool can't explain out of the grave and lay cash money to clear his debt.* Drinking. " 'Nother bourbon. You got any sugar for this water?" *Half my land. Can't support a family on half my land.* He fumbled in his pocket for leftover change; laid a quarter and odd pennies on the counter. They rolled from him. The bartender's hand caught them as they fell. A bottle sloshed over into his glass. He gasped as the next bourbon and sugar-water moved down. *I ain't drunk.* "I ain't drunk," he said. *So that's it. Well, now. Well, now.*

Burley looked up into the putty-colored face, saw no eyes, and asked for another drink. The piano played cheap music. *I have never been this drunk before,* he told himself, *never!* "I ain't never," he told the bartender. A hand was on his shoulder, and turning into the red-lighted room, Burley faced a man with a beer-stained tray. "I'm a landowner. A good farmer," Burley said. "Can't I have a little credit?"

He was on the sidewalk, following after another drunk. He pulled his pockets inside out, was surprised to find another coin, and in turning saw the world invert. He did not think of himself falling, it was the world that stood on end, left behind his back, slipping. The quarter fell from his flannel pocket. He reached for it and saw her feet in the mire of retch and sawdust. He lay on his back looking up into her putty face. *I could have found another nickel. Maybe he would have give me five-sixths of the bourbon and the sugar-water free.* He said to her, "You could have stayed to home." Her face came down to his; he could have sworn it was him rising, floating up through the ocher light past the ordered sequence of fallen earth, toward his resurrection and muse. She had a calico handkerchief. She wiped at the corner of his mouth. He pushed her away. "You could have stayed to home," he said.

He did not know when she had fled. He still searched out the quarter in the mire beside the boardwalk. He did not know he had reached the boardinghouse until the red fan above the door drew his eyes, and he stumbled up the steps to the veranda. He tried the door, and was amazed when it opened easily until he saw the shocked face of the matron in front of him, and then saw her white scrubbed hands waving in his face, saying, speaking, it seemed, from her hands, "You cannot enter here!" Daliah was unmoved, amazed. The woman held his arms. He pushed her away. "That there's my woman. She got my child in 'er."

Daliah drove them home. He saw her back from the rear boards of the wagon, the small defenseless back leaning from him into the moon-dappled September night. The wagon held him lightly. He felt no bumps or jolts; he did not even believe the bruises when they pained him the next morning. The one pain he did believe was seeing Daliah sitting in the wagon seat above him, untouched in the night, and pregnant too.

October came on them and his arrangements. The Monday after, he walked over his front forty, and looking back over his shoulder, saw the house recede. *God, but there ain't much of it left.* He saw how foreshortened and complete his farm was now, crossing the gate, and decided to give up the better bottom land beside the Salt River.

The old man, Breman, sat on his porch. Breman owned or held interest in a thousand acres in the county. He worked little himself; what was not left fallow he farmed on shares, tenancy, or upkeep if he was gracious and the land marginal.

Burley approached him. Breman drowsed, paunchy and long-faced, with bony arms inside soiled linens. Burley stopped.

"I see you, boy. Come on up here to the porch and I'll explain the line to you some more."

Burley walked up onto unpainted boards, which looked newly laid (probably one of Breman's tenants had worked off a debt by planing the porch boards into place). Burley pried mud from under his heel at the porch edge.

[77]

"You can even sit on one of my chairs for the explaining. What owning land won't get a man into!" Breman chuckled. "You think I like taking on another forty acres when I already got two hundred more than I can get shares for? I'd just as soon turn the most over to the government—the United States *federal* government, mind you—if I could figure a fair compensation for the time spent worrying over it. Hand me one of them apples." He took a blunt knife, whetted the blade stone, and peeled the apple, letting the curlings fall over the arm of the chair.

"What are you going to do with my forty acres?" Burley asked.

"Now, John, the sheriff was to have talked some of it over with you. I've no real interest in taking on that land. I'm doing you the favor."

"Then why didn't you settle for the front forty? You have the best of my land."

"And how was you thinking to keep this secret from that young wife of yours if I was to take interest on the acreage right outside her kitchen door? What'd you have her do? Walk halfway across your farm and then tell her: 'Now, Dali, it's all still mine, but I want you to start thinking that's not a boundary from the fence over.'" Breman smiled. "Why, you might as well pick up that house and move it over and hope when she opened the door she weren't seeing no difference."

"I don't want her to know," Burley said, reaching for an apple.

"Go ahead, it came from the tree on your property." Breman handed the knife to Burley.

"What's the terms?" Burley asked. "I got to know the terms."

Breman dropped his peels on the unpainted porch. He quartered the apple, cut a long curve out for the

[78]

core. Then he folded the knife and put it into his pocket. Burley shifted closer to hear.

"Fifteen years is all I will take. You work the farm same as usual. I take three quarters of the crop. The other quarter you put against buying the land back, against taxes and such. In fifteen years you have it back, deeded full."

"Only all my crop! You want I should wear laurel in my hair when I gather your tithe?"

Breman spit out a seed he had missed in the coring. He picked his teeth with an unclean thumbnail. He pointed the thumb in Burley's face. "I could have sold it the next day. I give you that promise. I won't sell the land from under you."

Burley stood suddenly, looking down into the old man's face. "You could be dead before another fifteen years."

"It's writ out," Breman said. He did not blink. He cored another apple. "Before you go would you mind picking up them peels and tossing them in the yard somewhere."

———

BURLEY WALKED ALONG THE RIVER'S EDGE. HE SHORED up against the high clay varve of the Salt River. *I didn't have to be married. I could have left the taxes unpaid myself and been right put up for the fifteen years. Now I got both. The easy thinking of not having to think and plan for fifteen years, and a wife I can lie to for fifteen years!* He left the river, passing the newly erected fence posts, worrying that he had not yet taken up a plow to cut a crop not to be his; worrying how to fill the four months lay-by before his prepaid fifteen years began. *I'll be thirty-four then. No, thirty-six. One year more than*

the start of the fifteen, plus fifteen, thirty-six I'll be.
He stepped into his house without remembering or
counting his footfall into the room where she sat. The
room was the color of churches: white-washed walls October sun-stained high on the boarding behind her. The
butternut-colored dress stretched across her. She was almost two now, already a duet with her child. With Burley's high-sounding voice they were almost three, a choir.

"I was figuring," he said. "Next year I'd better run
the bottom acres first. I'll run tobacco." He took a dipper from the bucket, poured water over his face and
shirtfront, drank his fill.

"You still ain't said she could come and stay till my
time," Daliah said.

He put the dipper back. "I don't mind her coming
when you birth," he said. "I can't abide Jaretta living
here for a month. You did say you have a month yet."

"More or less, I hear say," she said.

"When it's your time," he said.

She came slowly out of her chair, rising into the
October light above her head. It struck her face: the
choir had risen, taken color; the choir sang old songs.
"How will she know? Am I going to have to walk over
to Jaretta's and stand up on the porch banging on the
door, then tell her when she comes in her nightgown
and all to come on over? 'We got to walk back two miles
to my house so I can lay back in the bed and pull the
covers over me, and then you come in and pretend you
didn't see me arranging the sheets before you bring me
the baby.' "

"I said I would go for the doctor." Burley leaned
with both hands on the well bucket, seeing his un-
calmed face in the water.

"And that's better? I should have our bedding

room window open so Jaretta can hear my screams two miles away, and then when she gets here, tell her, 'Burley went for the doctor. But that's only four miles, twice as far as you, and he don't sleep with his windows open.' " The church light was on her face, red and somber like stained glass. "It's my first, Burl. I'm not knowing what to expect." She moved back to her chair, surrendering October to the walls again. "I need Jaretta . . . here."

Burley did not speak again. He put the bucket away. Jaretta Chapel came with a trunk the next morning.

JARETTA CHAPEL STEPPED DOWN OUT OF THE WAGON tugging at her baggage even before the carriage had completely stopped. Burley watched her from the breezeway, in the shadows behind the porch. She was a high-waisted girl, larger and stronger than Daliah, but with an easier, more assured stance, more aware of her own movement. She was a year older than Daliah, not yet married though she was engaged to a serious merchant, her second cousin, who owned a free section of land untouched by Breman. Burley watched as the trunk fell from the bed of the wagon, raising a small cloud of dust as it hit the ground. Daliah came out to the kitchen door beside him. "God's sake, go help her!"

In the morning it was a face very unlike Daliah's across the table. Jaretta sat high in the chair leaning forward in her low-buttoned dress. Stirring her coffee with a quiet abandon, she propped herself into his face.

"I asked Daliah to stay in bed. Her term is near over. It could be any time," she said.

[81]

"You an authority?" he said. He did not stir his coffee. He spooned sugar into it, letting it clot near the bottom, a surprise, sweet among the dregs.

She put her spoon down. "I saw two births before I was fourteen. I've helped at three others."

"Why don't you write to State University for your license?" he said.

She had a breakfast fixed, in one hand a plate with eggs and thin-cut bacon, in the other hand wellhouse-cold milk. She moved out of the breezeway, taking the dish over to the bedroom.

"Daliah can get up for her breakfast," he said. "I don't like your pamper on her."

Jaretta toed the door open. "Won't hurt none," she said.

Burley slept between the rooms in the breezeway warmth. Jaretta shared the bed with Daliah, saying when the time came, it was better for her to be at Daliah's side. "Besides, I can't be sleeping between chairs in the kitchen, nor on a pallet beside your bed. John, you go out to the barn or make a bed up on the porch. It's not cold yet."

He smelled the drifting wood smoke, heard her steps and the flow of cold water ringing into a roasting pan. Jaretta came to the door, her figure tall, prominent, accustomed. "Go get the doctor," she said.

He was astride the mule even before he remembered he had saddled the beast, and turned to see the tall glare of Jaretta Chapel behind him as he swung aside into the roadway. The sun was up. Shadows lay pale and drawn across his path. *My wife's bed even! Well, now, I only have to get the doctor. I don't even have to pretend I like what's she's doing for me.* Burley leaned the mule into a hurried lope that was not quite running. The mule was too surefooted to make haste just because Burley's great booted feet dug into its side. When he swung down again the second time, the doctor's carriage had already beat him back to the house. He stepped up into the hush. The doctor was putting away his instruments. Jaretta was at the window laying aside linen and throwing out the boiled water into the yard. She even smiled.

"Well, come on over and look at the baby."

Burley moved over to the bed. Daliah was drawn up small beneath sheets, sleeping again, quiet and damp in the November springlike morning.

"It's a girl," Jaretta said.

He pulled aside the coverlet and fumbled over the mound beside Daliah. He said to himself, *A girl. Well. That one's hers.*

The next four babies were strong-limbed sons. They were his. The children came easily and with less cultivation than his cash crops. He passed each succeeding year as fifteen minus one, minus two—never saying to himself that one year Nathan was born, or that John Jr. came the year corn was forty-five cents a bushel. Silas and Paul came so close together he had only one silent winter from September to May between their births before he could count one year's lay-by handed over to Breman. He made good crops; he made good sons. The doctor seldom came. Jaretta was now married and had her own birthing (Daliah had attended her), and with the remembrance of the actual pain, stood alone at all Daliah's birthings until the twins were born.

A sayer told them at six months there would be twins. Jaretta called for Daliah in her husband's bright painted carriage one afternoon. Burley, watching from the barn, did not know they had planned to go. Mattie, the oldest, nine years now, stood outside the fence waving as the carriage gathered its dust and rolled out of sight. She crossed the yard. Burley laid aside his hame string and gathered the girl into his hands.

"What's Batina Nuntee?" Mattie asked.

Burley turned her face up. "Where did you hear that name?"

"Mama and Aunt Jerry said they could drive there and back before it got dark."

He beat the mule beat the mule but it would not run. He was down into the trees beside the river before he remembered. He caught up the trace harness and righted the animal, and they came crashing out into the bright afternoon clearing high on a bluff. He pulled up, dismounted with a stumbling haste that threw him headlong through the dry grass. Hot and fierce in summer, the grass spiraled upward under his cleaving boot-steps. He came running *I can see it now I can see Jaretta make my wife blaspheme* striking at the door, throwing his fears loose and upward against the paintless frame. It did not give. It opened silently when his breathing was all that was left him, spent, furious, and asthmatic in the heat. Once inside he saw the alarmed face of his wife, Daliah, float up at him beside the amused, high, righteous face of Jaretta Chapel.

The room was near bare. There were no votive candles or burning lanterns, no beads or hangings. On one wall was a low shelf with four copper-colored jars; beneath it was the spectral head of Batina Nuntee. She was Negro, wore a pure white head rag. She may have been old. On the table was a headless chicken.

Mama Nuntee raised a hand, a palm outward, to him. The skin had the color of bleach and lye bath. She said, "There are two."

Burley stopped. The room was bright with the afternoon sun. "I will not have my fortune spoke to me over dead chicken flesh and mojo."

The Negro spoke again. "This chicken is my supper."

Then came Jaretta Chapel's high voice. "You fool!
This woman can tell. It doesn't take a chicken or magic
for Miss Nuntee to forecast what you have done out of
your own loins." Jaretta placed a long smooth hand on
Daliah's shoulder. "Why do you think I brought her? I
could almost tell."

"Jaretta Chapel, you—" Burley started.

"I said there was two," Batina Nuntee said again,
loud and less than arrogant, shattering Burley's unfinished curse. She reached across the table and placed both
hands over Daliah's womb. Daliah sat back in the chair,
not frightened, but resigned as if she had no say in the
matter, as if Jaretta Chapel and John Burley—and even
Batina Nuntee—had conjoined and conceived this baby
inside her and waited only for her fragile shell to fall
away from it and leave each of them with smug verifica-
tion. Mama Nuntee moved her hands lower on Daliah's
stomach. Her hands moved back. "There are two." She
turned on Burley. The black face spoke to him quickly,
honestly, and without error. "Beware, man. You gave
this child to her. Because you are a hard man, a man
will find breathing hard."

"What do you mean? What does she mean, Jaretta?"
Daliah said.

Mama Nuntee rose from her chair. She grasped the
headless chicken by the throat like a bottle. A gash of
blood was on the table. "You white folk get on out of
here. I got to fix this here chicken."

DALIAH NEVER SPOKE TO HIM OF THAT AFTERNOON, NOT
even when late in her term the doctor said the chance of

twins was great. Jaretta did not come over during the last months after Batina Nuntee had spoken, was not there the afternoon when the twins were born. The doctor held the children high for Burley to see. A boy; a girl. Burley named them Brett and Carlene, and laying them beside Daliah among the folds, he pulled the covers back over them and remembered the chances he took. He saw Batina Nuntee, holding the chicken to her slack breast, focusing sharply on the beautiful face of Jaretta Chapel, righteous and powerful and consumed with making his wife, Daliah, live in rooms other than his own. Maybe that was why, when he looked down at the two sleeping children, over the sleeping face of his wife, he believed the siring was Jaretta Chapel's—that the seducing of Daliah from his simple life was a plot consummated between the small-boned face of Daliah Faye Brownlee and the high-sounding woman called Jaretta Chapel. He sat up tall in his cloistered, church-colored walls and breathed. He had two more children. He had six more years to gather and lie, lie and regather to his name his land's redemption. How could he explain it to her, to his Daliah/Jaretta? He picked up a baby. It was his son, sleeping in his massive-boned hands. He turned the child and saw in the face his own likeness, and he said to himself, quite loud into the booming silence of the afternoon, "She had nothing to do with this." He repeated the words again when a month later Daliah ran screaming from the house with Brett clutched to her breast.

The screaming came from under the mimosa. Daliah was a swift-moving blur along the forever muslin fences, drowning under the burr of bees swarming on fallen pears. Burley stood fixed in the doorway of the shed, broken harness in hand, and saw her pitching toward the road. He moved to cut her off. She outdistanced him, throwing over her shoulder a white face, moving haltingly away. He caught her, dropping the hame in the dust and pears. She fell to her knees, backward onto her haunches. Brett was still pressed to her breast. She let him slip down onto her slack thighs, peaceful, dead, and close-held.

AFTER, LYING IN BED BESIDE DALIAH ABOVE THE DISTURBED ground, he thought, *She's got nothing on dying.* He had not touched Daliah yet. The thinking was the same, was a memory.

The cemetery was quite full when they buried Brett. Interment was simple. A few neighbors rode the high summer dust and lifted half-spadefuls (a half-spade was all they were allowed; the hole was not large enough for them all to get a chance at spading their grief), watched the dust laid over. Jaretta Chapel came too. She stood by herself near the headstone of Burley's father, in a correct and meticulous black dress, no veil. She had her best gloves; did not lift a requisite half-spadeful. She moved warily. A carriage rolled swiftly along the fence. Heads turned. Batina Nuntee drove by. Jaretta moved farther from them. Daliah sat on a stool brought out for her into the shade. She took Carlene's weight upon her thighs, sitting unmoved and close-held unto herself. Burley had not touched her since Brett died. Daliah dropped one compressed wad of clay into the grave. They could see her fingers pressed into the clay roll, heard it rattling over the yellow box, thrown almost with contempt. She took Mattie's hand. Their four sons followed behind her.

Wagons rolled away. Boards and wheel springs complained into ruts. Burley counted the cloth-covered

[87]

dishes placed on a sawhorse table in the yard. He could not think. He counted them again, saying to himself, *That's gooseberry.*

Jaretta Chapel spoke to him. Now he would not have to try at thinking. She was behind him.

"Dali said when you took him from her arms all you said was, 'What about Carlene?' " Jaretta moved to his side. "Have you so many sons that you lose count when one of them dies?" she said.

Burley's arm tightened. *God, I could have struck her.* Tense muscles relaxed. He did not remember turning to face her. She was almost as tall as he. They could look one another in the eye. He saw a bare hand ride between them. She had taken off one of her fine black gloves. The hand touched his too closely shaven face.

He said, "I have five sons."

The hand fell away, surrendered the air between them. She put her glove back on, putting fine long fingers in place, tucked and stretched behind the skin of good leathers. She straightened her hair. Her carriage came abreast of him, moving slowly.

"I brought the gooseberry," she said.

IN THREE YEARS THEY HAD ANOTHER SON. DALIAH HAD not wanted the baby, had said as much. "Here I sit and it's not even my making." She sat in a straight-backed chair against the kitchen wall. The kitchen was filling with chairs, eight now. "Haven't you had enough? You got to bring more on me!"

Burley switched aside the last of his harness repair. He closed his whetted knife. "What we've done." His words were like spittle. "How many times have we lain together in twelve years? Thousands? We didn't get no children out of every one of them thousands. I can't be knowing which time."

"We can't afford another baby!" she said. "What makes you think surviving can be stretched into another mouth? Seems you can't make a decent crop on eighty acres."

"I've plowed, I've—"

"I had some arithmetic in school too. I can read about yields." She brought an almanac from the folds of her skirt. "Or haven't you read this?"

He took the book from her hands, rolled it between frustrated fingers. He shook. It was not that he did not believe her. He saw the fall of her form, the color of her face.

"What are you planning to throw into the grave after him?" he said quickly. He put the almanac in his rear pocket.

"The first bushel of corn past feeding this family," she said.

Burgess was born, and even that did not change their days. Burley cared for the baby. She did not neglect the child—she nursed and diapered him—but there was no attachment. It was Burley's large man hands that held the child close. He had to. She said the boy was his.

He worked in his corn, and coming suddenly in on her half-lit kitchen, saw that the column of figures she read were corn prices. She laid the paper aside, and he left without eating, plowing until sundown as on the first day. The next day, an April hotter than June air, trying to show one of his sons the work, he came upon her again. She had been sewing. Muslin sheets were muddled about her arms. He did not understand her look. So he plowed. Fifteen years had passed. The crop was his own, and as he came, striding fast at sundown

[89]

through his blameless corn rows, he did not hesitate as he stepped through the fence, nor turn back to see how much he was gaining back to his name. That night when he bedded her, moving over and wallowing in the damp repetition of her tears, he thought of his proud intact acreage, how good the crop was going to be made of fine seeds coming up—moving over; planting seeds.

———

BURLEY TURNED OUT OF HIS SLEEP, TURNED OUT OF A morning without cock crow. There was no clatter from the kitchen. Perhaps she had stepped out the back door for another armload of kindling, telling himself as he rose, still sleep-laden and moving catlike, "If Nate didn't load the fire box last night I'll have his bottom red." He searched beside the bed for his boots, his white-socked feet whispering around the bedding before he remembered he had left his boots at the kitchen door. Reaching for them, coming across the warm breezeway, he smelled no fire, and already had one boot on before he clumped limping and distracted over to the pot iron cookstove. He removed a lid. Ashes. The box beside the stove was filled with wood scraps.

The room was dark, the shutters had not yet been thrown back from the high inset windows. He opened them, and the light fell in. The dishes were as she had left them, washed and stacked on the drainboard. The dishrag was stretched dry across the pump handle. He stomped his other foot into the iron-hard boot. He was out the back door, frightened and alone, hurt almost, in the great morning dew. High running furrows ran from the door. Beside the well head he found the folded muslin sheets. He gathered them in his hands. The stench of dew-wet cloth carried up. It smelled nothing like the hand that had sewn them.

He towered quietly beside Mattie's bed. Mattie was fifteen and looked like her mother, and in the dark he almost believed it was Daliah who had slipped into their daughter's bed. He thought back, *I was no rougher last night.* Shaking Mattie's shoulder, he said, "Girl, you got to get up now."

"Daddy?"

"Don't wake the others till they want to get up." He drew the covers over her slender legs, smoothed the sheets beside her. "Your mama and I got to go over to Jaretta Chapel's. Dali's waiting in the wagon out front," he lied. "There's side meat set out, and bread. Fix breakfast with what you find."

"Daddy?" He turned back from the door. She had sat up, stretching. "Ask Priscilla if she found my red hair ribbon. I think I lost it in the back of their carriage after Wednesday prayer."

He had no thoughts of red ribbons, coming down off his red mare and up onto the wide veranda of the Chapel house. The house was Victorian, newly built, white clapboard with railings and moss roses. The porch had been recently painted. In the morning heat the boarding was tacky beneath his boots. He stood there in front of the door, looking down, thinking he had carried something up onto the veranda under his feet, when the door opened.

Jaretta Chapel had her arms folded across her bosom. She wore a dressing gown long to her feet. Hair was about her shoulders, and her face was already painted, or left painted from the night before: bold-colored lips. She said, "The painters just took down the roping yesterday."

"Where is she?" he said.

She pushed her hair behind her ears, flinched, and shrugged slightly. "I would say who, but there's only one woman what you would miss if she wasn't there to put coffee in your hands." She pulled one side of her hair back down. "Dali isn't here."

"Where did you send her?"

"Send her?" She laughed and stepped back from the door, looking over her shoulder into the still dark house. She said, low, a whisper almost, "You aren't kidding. Dali's gone. What did you do to her?"

He was leaving the porch, was up on the horse before she could come across the veranda and out into the yard and catch up on the bridle. He looked down on her. "We're accusing each other of wronging on her. She's gone. I don't know where," he said.

She let go of the horse. "John Burley, you let me know."

He was down off the horse a dozen times about the town, throwing out his question and without waiting on an answer throwing himself back onto the sweated flesh, to spur and come down one final time in front of the county jail. The sheriff was a proper lawman. He wore a fat black gun at his side, too heavy for his size. Some voters had grumbled some eighteen years back he could not hold his own, until he had single-handedly brought down a prisoner with the handle of a spade across the face in the middle of the square. The sheriff had had four men pick the prisoner up and carry him back to jail.

"Did you quarrel with her?" the sheriff asked.

"We don't quarrel," Burley said.

The sheriff sat to his table in front of the barred windows. The sun lay flat across the glass. Stripes were on the table, stripes over his hands.

"Did you hit her?"

"I never hit her."

"How do you know she's gone? Not just about the place or to the neighbors?"

"She's gone," Burley said.

Coming down off the hills above the river, he left the track only once, cutting wide around the cultivated fields of Batina Nuntee. He could have sworn oath she stood behind a tree waiting for him; her laughter was on the breeze. On that one huge hill, overgrown with weeds, yellow with the mustard heads that grew behind his barn, he saw the bright painted wheels of Jaretta Chapel's carriage against the dull paintless gray of his sheds. "Done brought her home!" he said aloud. Jaretta Chapel was in his kitchen, kneeling to tie the laces of Silas's shirtfront, letting him out of her hands to run past Burley's legs and out the door. Jaretta's hair was drawn back. Her face was unadorned. *It was last night's paint*, he thought.

"Did you find her?" Jaretta asked.

"Didn't you bring her home!" Burley said.

"Why are you so sharp-tongued!" Jaretta loomed out of the closeted space of the kitchen.

"I have suffered you in my house, in her life—"

Jaretta would not flinch. "I have made Dali better," she cut in. "I knew her father, her brothers and sisters who could not wait to get out from under his hands." She circled the table, taking up linen and breakfast bowls. She lay them in the basin beneath the pump. "I warned her about you. That very day at the church when you came up to her, and me, and your sister." Jaretta pumped the handle. She quit just as water came from the spigot. "Don't think she didn't confide how you stood in the side lot, holding a tadpole-filled water bucket when the shot went off over your head." She was laughing. "But that's all right." She pumped again. Water came over her hands. She wiped at the corner of her eye, then took one of Daliah's aprons and dried her hands. "We women have that much over you. We do our foolishness in secret, carrying on and crying and raving in kitchens. But you men, well, you men do your disasters in public, drinking in bars right on the town square, and then riding fast horses over half the county, leaving gossips everywhere you set down off the horse about how your wife left you."

"I never said she left me," Burley said.

"What do you think they'll all think? What? That she's off for her health, taking a summer's leisure at the seashore?"

"You can't mouth in my house how I keep my family."

"I've been midwife to your crowd," she ˙said. "I pulled six of your babies from Dali's womb!" She shook. "Who has better right?"

He wanted to strike her, even had his hands raised, but finding air around him and a distance across the table which he knew Jaretta had cleaned with her very hands, he was without power. Again she did not flinch as he came around the table, taking her arm and wordlessly moving to the door. She did not resist him—until they reached the door. She would not be put out. Her sweet odor was in his face. He knew his own sweat, his worked flesh, lathered and bedded.

Mattie was stepping onto the porch. She looked over them both, moved past, wire skirted and moving coltishly, and sat to the table. Her hands were laid flat.

"My God, but you better watch that girl!" Jaretta said. "She's more guts than either one of us—any three

[94]

of us." Jaretta lay a hand on the girl's head. "Maybe Daliah birthed it all away—gave the most fortitude to Mattie. Then she ran for lack of guts."

Jaretta gathered her bag, gave one final objective look around the room to see if she had left something undone. Burley did not walk her to her carriage. He heard the complaint of springs, saw the red wheels pivot into the curved ruts from the barn into the road. He did not think of her again.

"Where's Mama?" Mattie asked.

"She went over to Jaretta Chapel's."

"Aunt Jaretta said she was in town with you."

Mattie still sat at the table, with the wide flat hands laid out. Already at fifteen she was larger than Daliah, had carried the fine-boned delicate features into a larger likeness.

"Your mother's not in town," he said finally. And then he said, logically and without lying, "She had to leave."

"Indiana is a far ride by train," Mattie said. "How many sisters does Mama have in Indiana?"

Indiana, he thought. *Yes. The only people she has.* "She went to Indiana to visit her sister."

"How long do you think I'll have to watch the kids while you ride after to help Mama back?" Mattie said.

SO HE WAS NOT SURPRISED TO BE RIDING NORTH. HE WOULD not have been more surprised if Mattie had had his horse already tied and provided for at the front of the house. He brought out two tow sacks, attached them to the saddle with the dried meat, hard bread, and dried apples (Mattie said, "Them sweets can keep a person satisfied"). He rode far into the dark because he did not think of stopping (Mattie had not told him to get down off the horse and lay down until dawn), and after one it was raining. He took shelter in a barn beside the road. The air was awash in calico-stained smells—yellow rotted corn, mildewed hay grasses, rotted birchwood. He had come too far to sleep. He lay in a damp corner against the wind; beneath his shoulder he felt the give of planking in the storm. He ate two hard biscuits. Then he remembered. He popped one of the dried apples between his teeth. He sucked on it a minute, then spit it into the dark at his feet. *I wished she'd put in a tin of them peaches instead.*

In the morning water flowed in roadside ditches. The ruts in the road were silver with rain. He splashed up onto the horse. Near noon he came across tracks. He looked down a tunnel floored in chert, colored blue by the rain. The rails were shiny. He turned down them. He did not eat.

The water station came up on his right. One man worked inside. Weathered and red-faced, the station man offered him coffee. It was afternoon.

"Any passenger trains heading north yesterday would have gone up through Madison over into Indiana," he answered. "You want some dried fruit with that coffee?"

"You got peaches?"

"I got apples," the man said.

Burley studied the map spread between them on the high western-lighted ledge. "Can I get up this road and across?"

"Let me see." The station man traced a pudgy finger down a red line. "The train curved over." He pushed his finger across and off the page. "But if you was to make any time on that train, there's a ferry at

Vevay. Stay on the road. At Ghent they can get you across."

"What time did the train go over into Indiana?"

"Hard to say. And what with the storming—I mean I got a tree down over to New Liberty!"

The rain blew as he left the station. By night the road disappeared under a brown slime. Burley doubled against the horse's neck. He saw only the rising foot plod of the left front leg. *She didn't tell me I would need a hat.* He thought he heard a train, that howl of round steel meeting railed steel, but he had left the curve of the tracks miles behind. He watched the horse's front legs, saw the brown swirl deepen about its flank, and looking up, saw white caps and froth. The horse had walked into the river.

He fought to bring her back, stood straight in the saddle and reined to come about. A fallen tree floated silently by, spun in front of the horse, throwing its green leaves on the gray water. The horse balked, raised up out of the water, and fell back. Burley saw the hooved legs cleave the sky as the horse's rear quarters surrendered to the mud and drew them down into the water. The horse was on top of him now. Burley's leg was tangled in the stirrup. *There wasn't no way for her to know it. The mare won't swim, I ought to have knowed it.* The tree came to face him. It bore square. He went underwater. The roots scraped along his back, thudded against the bank, and peeled down his back again. *She didn't say I would have to breathe all the time.* He came up to the surface. The horse was gone.

In the morning he woke to the sound of running water. He did not remember where he was. *Them biscuits sat right bad in my stomach. I'll get Dali to make a tonic, something with mint in it.* He turned his head. Mud closed over his lips. He sat up spitting. Before him

[97]

the high Ohio River paled, wide, cloud shrouded. He could not see the other bank. The horse moved nearby, chewing on grass at the river's edge.

In an hour the sky overhead cleared. Clouds stood defeated on the northern bank. The sun was out briefly. He washed his face in a puddle; saw his bruised face in the still pool, ill defined—fine gold cheeks under a three-day beard. He had no eyes.

In another hour he was hungry. He moved to the horse, searched for the left saddlebag, found it thrown, water-rifled, far up on the bank. The biscuits and dried meat were gone. He still had the apples. *Well, now. Mattie must have prayed some over them apples. Well, now.* He chewed them slowly, spitting out the roughage he could not set his teeth to. Soon he had a pile of apple bits between his boots. He tried spitting the hard spots onto the mound, made a game of it, and was mad when the apples gave out. He ground them under his heel.

Across the river he could see where the ferry had been. A number of wooden buildings lay flattened to the ground. *Well, now,* he thought again. *It must have been a tornado I heard.* A large flatboat was driven into the bank. A few smaller craft littered the shore farther up. He thought he saw a ribbon of rope flailing downstream into the current. He watched men come down from the heights above the landing. He called—knew they could not hear him—waved. They must have seen him. They waved a large yellow cloth. He sat down to wait.

He had the whole day to think. *I can give her at least one day to say she was just visiting.* He looked at the apples twice; turned from them twice. He did not build a fire to dry out. There was no tinder in the swim of mud. He had no matches. He did not smoke.

Through the day he watched the far shore, saw the piecemeal come together under the hands of men he feared were northerners. The flatboat claimed their attention. Hammering rang out through the morning. At noon they raised a splash as the men carried the ferry back into the river. Burley saw them sit down to eat, spreading the yellow standard on the high ground above the water—water like his sweat, like the Salt River floods, and until two days ago, like the dishwater his wife had thrown out the back door.

He could still see her hands, small and delicately veined and etched into the light study of her apron, pale, crystalline under the beaded outline of pan water. Hands lay close held and equal over her hips where the hush of her thighs gathered and spent something furious and molten. The swirl of her bosom receded, recalled as if she was forever catching her breath, sucking, and buttermilk in flavor. But he knew that was the taste of her lips, sadly parched because she could not nurse of herself that milk of dun-colored breast he knew as the quiver under his hand in the dark. He knew her by touch. The contour, the tuck . . . and the smell; washed, faded flesh rose beneath his nostrils in a woman-flood. And in turning aside after, was the presence beside him in the dusk, that dip behind his back in the mattress where her crying had ceased. She was the dark-headed growth beside him in the April morning light, stilled, turned away from him, grainy and kinetoscopic as he saw her rise, lift herself unindulged into and across the breezeway. And once, just once he remembered seeing her turn back to look at him, and her face was drawn into detail by the door, her half-face, chiaroscuro and pigmented, a struck liberty coin face chiseled and silver. For a moment her mouth came to him with a smile, not at him—they already had five children—but was a quick flash of teeth already sucking air; drawing her morning dishwater and breathing above it; the intake, the quick splash and sucking . . .

. . . the sucking flatboat rose on long poles and splashed. Burley looked up. The rear tiller rose and cut as the boatman turned and drifted the craft into the bank. The man was larger than Burley. He drew the pole high out of the water and thrust it out at Burley.

"Grab holt," he said.

The man stepped down. The boat rose in the river. He was dressed in coarse military cloth. "Can that horse take to the water? The ferry will take much work. And I told the boys I couldn't wait watching you sit this side of the river on us." The boatman uncoiled a length of green wet rope, and was surprised to see Burley sitting the horse.

"Throw up the rope," Burley said. "She might of walked into the river in the dark. The water will hit her across the chest and she'll turn."

The boatman poled the craft from the faded bank, came up fast with each shift and down-sinking of his sapling pole. Burley lay tight over the mane of the horse, one hand cupped through the side harness. He buried his fingers in the nostrils, buried his whitened hand over the horse's breathing to calm it. He clucked into the horse's laid-back ears. The animal's eyes were like broken porcelain. The horse bounced like a buoy. In two strokes Burley laid his hands on the boarding, and lifted himself up and sprawled wet booted and sneezing.

"Got some good decent whiskey to the other side," the man said.

"I've no taxes to pay this time," Burley said.

"Was some storm!" The boatman poled to one side. The sun flickered between his legs. "It wasn't like we didn't see them clouds pile up over into Kentucky. The wind blew all afternoon. When it was dark we couldn't see the trees bent to the ground no more." The boatman swallowed. He poled to the other side. The sun flickered again. "My wife, she don't understand how I came down to work." He stopped poling. "The girl was caught in the storm." The shaft trailed in the river, reflecting broken and illusioned away from his hands. "What was I to do? Stay to home and help dress her in white for tomorrow?" The boatman poled again as the river grew shallow over sand near the Indiana shore. "Women don't understand."

"Is that Indiana?" Burley said.

"Wait," he said. "She was wearing her white dress."

The horse swung past, bobbing out of the water. The boat lurched. Burley released his line. The horse plodded through storm-rent weeds and clay-covered rocks. The horse found roots to chew farther up the bank.

The boatman shook his head.

"I got to pay for the trip," Burley said. "Can I help with the work then?"

"A man what waits a night and a day in the mud can't have no time to be offering."

The bank was steep. Burley cut closer to the landing. The boatman walked in front of the mare, stopped and said upward into the horse's face, "I hope you find her."

"What?"

"It's always a woman," he said.

THE ROAD WAS CLEAN AND FIRMLY LAID. THAT KENTUCKY-blue haze was replaced by a motionless green taffetalike crispness. Towns seemed of less purpose, scattered by chance where homesteading men dropped from wagon beds with clean sharp axes and began life north of the river. Farms were small, quiet behind split rails rather than white board fences. Burley saw hog farms and corn-cribs as he rode. He asked directions twice—once from a straight-haired old man scything pigweed from a road-side ditch, who pointed an arthritic forefinger farther up the same path to the growth which was Canaan, In-diana; and once in Canaan, stopping before a white bell-towered church. He came through the church doors in the afternoon, trod the red and maroon floor where the sun played with a high-set stained-glass window, and asked the organist, practicing the startled, dying chords of "At the Cross," the way to his sister-in-law's farm.

Side roads came together, crossed, came apart, and slipped into less than paths. He could see the house set far back in the wooded field, and from the wind he smelled a tended fire below lye pots. He turned in be-tween powerful cut fences, passing on his left the plotted furrows he knew would be corn, thinking, *My crop will best that any year.* He stopped abruptly in front of the house and sat long on the back of the mare. *Do I call her out or wait for her to happen out the door and watch her mouth fall open like she was eating too hot banana pepper?*

He sat the horse a full five minutes, counting them out in his head. His legs ached. He had ridden the horse without rest since the ferry. *Maybe she'll be out the back door. At least her sister would let her throw the very dishwater out that cleans the plate she ate from.* The house was square, the windows evenly set and many paned in the side walls. The ground sloped beneath rank and as yet uncut jimson and foxtail. A new-honed scythe lay on its side among the weeds. He had a path close to the side boarding; and sitting high on his horse he was level with the windows, and saw between close handmade lace curtains the sepia parallax of the room from one unlit corner. As he passed, he twisted his head over his shoulder, and a far corner came to him with highboys, brass beds, rugs, and one prismatic crystal lamp on a table in the center of the room. Sunlight from the front of the house hued the walls in green and red and violet. Sheds and a trelliswork of beans ran from the back of the house. The horse stepped high over chickens. A lone spotted bird dog barked at him from a pen.

The girl sat in the sun on a bench beside the rear porch. She had a corncob and clay doll layered in blue-washed calico and lace like the curtains. The doll had corn-silk hair; the girl's hair was dark, and one side was braided. She worked on the other.

The shadow of the horse fell across the bench. She pulled the doll close behind her. She said, "There ain't none of them home."

"I'm looking for a woman. Your Aunt Dali?" Burley said.

"No, sir. We ain't seen no relatives up here. It's planting time. Everybody's busy. 'Cept Uncle Jack— that's Daddy's brother. He works the next farm over. We see him all the time. He don't work none too hard or busy no way."

Burley sat quietly. The horse took a step forward. Burley stepped her back.

The girl worked the braids of her hair, was having pains. The girl undid the hair again. She flexed her hands. "I can't seem to get my fingers laid into it right," she said.

Oh, my God, he thought. *Oh, my God.* He smelled the lye strongly now. The girl had tended the fire: her bare prints ran back and forth between the bench and the kettle. His boots smothered her prints as he knelt beside the girl. She did not cringe, did not draw back her heavy lidded eyes when he reached toward her hair. His hands did not shake, but there was a flutter in his heart, the quick respiration as he saw his very own hands separate her thin hair, thinking, *I have two daughters. I do have two daughters.* He could smell her lye ashes and calico sweat. Her doll watched them, the clay cheeks rouged and muddy, hollow black eyes framed beneath rotting corn-silk hair. The smells—corn and lye and ash.

"There hasn't been another woman here? About your mother's age?" he asked.

"No, sir. Except the church ladies. They want Mama to bring the deviled eggs." The girl fingered the completed rows above his hands, felt if Burley was doing fair, was pleased. "It's the mustard. Mama likes right much mustard in her deviled eggs."

Burley backed away, withdrew his fingers from the mist of her hair, and was stepping back into the stirrup when he turned back down to speak to her.

"Did I get the braid tight enough?"

"Yes, sir," she said, placing her hands flat aside her ears. "You must have practiced some."

"Horse's mane," he said.

He turned the horse around, putting aside the small sphere which broke in his heart (he told himself it was not finding Daliah), putting aside that touching fever of a girl's hair, and beside the house's square window again—the room was violet and green alone now—paced himself because he knew he must not turn to see her again. He heard feet, bare on clay and uncut grass, circling the house on the far side. He came to the corner and the girl's pigtails vanished beside the front veranda; a giggling braid song. He breathed again, sitting high on the horse between the powerful gates, erected himself, and came into Canaan for the night and whiskey; drank both from a cut-crystal glass; and dreamed; and cried that he could not relish braiding Mattie's and Carlene's soft hair. Daliah Faye Brownlee wore combs.

(HE LOOSENED THE COMBS, RETRIEVED THEIR ALABASTER sparkle from her hair. He touched her; she did not tremble, or flinch under his sliding hands. He did not even know the words he hissed into her ears behind the loosened hair as he tasted the gravel coarseness of her sunburned throat against his dry mouth. She pushed him away, lifted his head; he could see her threatened face curve from him like the silver back of a spoon. A hand drew across his lips, was pressed searching and insistent against his teeth. His nostrils flared; her hands smelled of lye and corn flour; the white starch of her corn powders was luminous in the curving away face, and barren and unsinging cheekbones made hollows under his fingers, searching that same for her mouth, to caress and take bites from it. But he lost her face. Her head had turned to the side to curse into the chinaberry rustle of split percale, turned and strained until his hands held only the untied hairs of her neck, tracing down and tasting the corn starch, choking against her odor) choking, vomiting his dream over the side of the bed into the red-ringed rim of the Canaan chamber jar.

IN THE MORNING HE RODE AGAIN AFTER A SOFT BREAKFAST of eggs and slightly sweet milk, passed the ditches of scythed pigweed. He had been to Canaan, had passed

[105]

through, returned, slept, and left. He had made no miracles, had not come upon her amazed eyes and questioning mouth as if he could have told her to get up on his mare. *Maybe I should have rode me an ass,* he thought, smiling. He made the ferry road by midday. But coming up silently above the hills among the gathered moss, he saw, and turned in at the iron gates. The funeral was already settled. They had come out of the houses, and gathered and frowned and wept in the unpainted walls of a boarded church, and carried the white lace carefully and without many steps to the side yard. Mourners stretched from the steps of the side door. The gravesite was not far from the walls and some few of them still stood on the steps as Burley stood down. He retreated to the stiff eaves of a pine tree, breathed in its scent of clay and wood; he tried not to remember. Across the mound the boatman offered with a tilted back head as if to say, "She would not let me work the boat today. Today I got to remember whether I can, or even care. And thank you."

Burley moved away, smelled his own fierce welling throat. *Damn her, I can't need her so!* and knew that was not right. Not having her for fifteen years and seeing the way she stood in each doorway watching him come up out of the same yellow clay which they carried over when they buried Brett. He saw her still, sitting beside his other sons and with Carlene placed on her slack thighs, watching her throw one compressed clay handful over the tallow coffin.

He did not need to watch his carelessly placed footfalls among country crosses, or the bending and the retrieving, nor moving in line as he passed the clay cut. He faltered, like he was seeing Daliah's hand reach from under his own, and saw the soft yellow lump dismiss his fingers and plop like hardened honey.

No one asked him by what right he rode large-boned horses into their funerals where a white-dressed girl left them to grieve too close to a church wall, the church where that same girl in that same dress had carried and dropped sweaty brass coins into the offering. They passed him unnoticed with their pressed and collarless starched shirts and simple linsey-woolsey gray dresses and broad shoes laced about their grieving ankles.

The boatman stood among the pines, seething as he watched each and every one come and dispose of their dirts—and the one he cared to see was Burley, who last and without justification extended his hand and did not smile. They shook. Burley came up on the horse again, and moved away, out of the gates into the running swift currents and smells of a river after a storm.

"Do you see her sitting the horse behind me?"

"You didn't find her."

"You think I pushed her a ways back—made her walk the same as she left? She wasn't in Indiana."

"Oh," Jaretta said.

Burley mounted the steps. He moved to the door, but saw the broom leaning against the frame. He untied his boots and dropped them at the sill.

"You're keeping my house right neat, Jaretta Chapel," he said. "Did you make up mine and Dali's bed, we left it in such a pile."

"A house gets dirty in four days."

"Was you training Mattie what to look for under the beds?"

"John," Jaretta said. She was in the doorway after him, calm, a part of the woodwork. Her hair was down, perfectly uncombed and under a head rag. "I don't know what you'll be needing, what you'll have to make for the kids. I'm not interested in the sound of your bedsprings."

Burley passed his eyes beyond her; he was not gracious.

"I've some cold potatoes and a half chicken set by," Jaretta said.

"The springs make right much noise," he said.

The chicken broke open before him on a cold plate. The potatoes were tasteless and like paste. He ate them. Jaretta was not far out of the kitchen. He heard her calling the children, but he did not see them come in, or arrange themselves in front of the table, in a quiet group shooshed by the flapping of Jaretta's apron. It was Daliah's apron she wore. One of Daliah's best.

"John," Jaretta said.

He took another bite, gripped the bread between his fingers, and sponged at the hard gravy. The gravy would not take to the bread. He did not want to miss any of the gravy.

Mattie said, "Daddy—" She looked down over the children, her hand on Carlene's head. "Was Mama having a good visit to Indiana?"

Burley stopped chewing. He swallowed. The bread would not go down. He coughed.

"Your Mama . . . your Mama's not visiting into Indiana," he said finally. He ate another corner of bread. They watched him drink buttermilk.

"Oh, Daddy," Mattie said.

He stopped her. "Now, your Mama is a careful woman. She can . . . she can . . ." He did not know what to say. These were his children. He had given them life and bathed them, carried them on his shoulders, placed rifles in his oldest sons' hands and told them when to pull, had pulled covers over them in the night when he had found them naked as the Kentucky winter passed the thin house walls. He did know them.

"I think Mama's hiding some'ere," Burgess said.

"No," Burley said.

"Yes," said Mattie. She turned Burgess and faced him, getting down on her knees. "Mama's playing games. She's good at hide-and-seek. We just haven't found where she's hid yet. We're just not playing the game very well, are we, Daddy? Are we, Aunt Jerry?"

Jaretta was white. She fanned herself with the apron, bringing the shallow April heat to her and over her head. "Best player I've ever seen," she said.

"Let Daddy eat now," Mattie said. "You boys go out now."

"Pa," John Jr. said. "I'll put up the horse. I'll comb her down too."

Burley nodded to his son. "Give her some apples. She's taken a liking for apples."

The children were like mirrors, trailing with Mattie at the end of the line. She turned, silhouetted in the doorway. Burley could not see her face. It was afternoon and the sun was white off the wall behind her. She moved on.

Burgess ran back by the door. He crouched down by the hinges. He said, "Daddy, I ain't going to look for her no more. Mama doesn't play fair." Burgess ran on, clattered off the porch, and screamed into the sun-bright yard.

"It will do for now," Jaretta said. She took off the apron, folded it across a chair. "What will you tell them next week? Next month?"

"She'll be back before then," Burley said. The chicken made him sick.

"Will she?" Jaretta snapped. She brought her face close. He realized she was sitting at the table with him.

"Can you count on her? What makes you think she hasn't quit you for good, gotten rid of your silence and hard times?"

"I've tried," he said.

"Yes, you have tried, but what happened? We haven't had bad times since they speculated silver. But you never got better, you who have eighty of the best Salt River acres in the county. You have fine sons coming up to work—my God! Let Nathan have a year and you can field three teams of mules out for plowing." Jaretta was right in his face. He could smell her toilet. She had not forgotten her colognes. "Daliah's been waiting for fifteen years. I think she's been right patient. You could have made something by now."

He wanted to tear into the tin box where he kept his legals. To show the very paper written on and claused, and with Breman's own hand laced across the bottom, higher and larger than his own crimped penning, John B. Mead. He would not.

"I did not ask you to audit my bank ledger," he said.

"If your ledger's like your heart you're probably bankrupt," she said.

He had kept the secret for fifteen years, for fifteen years he had counted his anniversaries; each year the burden had become lighter, saying to himself, *Just so many more years left. I can hold her off another few years.* Somehow he had persevered with the lying, owed no explanation, and certainly had no reason to explain to Jaretta Chapel. He did not even like Jaretta Chapel.

He did not see Jaretta to the door that evening. He had already turned his horse-tired legs onto the mattress. He heard the door close across the breezeway. The next day he did not see much of her—he plowed; he was a week behind almost—nor in the weeks that followed, and into the summer when he was up out of his corn, sowing purple-hulled peas between the rows. Not even when the morning glories sprouted instead and grew wild and beautiful everywhere between the seed corn, did he stop and say morning or evening to her. Paul and Nathan brought lunch out to him. Out to the barn or into the fields as Daliah had done.

It was not that he was unthinking of Daliah. For a month he saddled his horse in the morning and called the sheriff out onto the boardwalk and asked. The sheriff did not give him hope. At first the sheriff came barefoot out onto the walk, then by the second week the sheriff just opened the front shutters and spoke outward through the green-painted bars, yellow striped in the too-early morning. Burley sent many telegrams. He could not afford them. But he sent them to relatives and her distant kin. They all came back the same, words without even the shadow of Daliah Faye Brownlee behind. By July he stopped sending telegrams. He knew no one else to ask. He spoke to the sheriff only once a week now—when in town on a Saturday, or when he passed the badge riding the violent dust about the county in a brown-stained carriage.

In August the corn was high. The morning glories stunted in the parallel shade. He slept later in the morning. He sometimes woke to the horse moving in her stall, puzzled that Burley no longer rode her fast in the morning. He woke that one day running his hands over the side of the bed into the hollows where she had lain. He rolled his fist into the curve of her hips, stroking and smiling. He made believe she was not gone, that their bed was empty only for a short time—perhaps she had not come to bed just yet. He believed easier that she had not come, rather than admit she would have left cold sheets. He smelled coffee. Outside he heard birds, shrill and fighting. He rolled over, leaving behind the hollows and the needs and came barefoot across the breezeway, ignoring the splinters and the cold boards. The kitchen door was propped open with a table bench. Kindling flames lapped the bottom of the coffee pot. Shutters had been thrown open. The sun battered the fragile, loved furnishings, the metal pans, piecemeal flatware, and a number of chipped glasses set in order around the table. He heard kindling split, turned and saw a woman's back slip behind a corner of the smoking shed. His heart faltered, caught up on itself and shut his breathing. The grass was wet, all dew and silver among the rank weeds below clowning birds in the trees. His bare feet didn't admit the chill. Beside the smoke shed his feet hit the dust of the yard and were caked and soled with earth. The woman swung the axe again.

"Dali?"

She turned and spoke to him, "Daddy?"

Mattie dropped the axe.

"I'm sorry, Daddy, it's one of her old dresses," she said.

And she was gone, had gathered her split wood to her breast. The axe lay against the shed, the handle worn, the head rusty at the stave, but with a blade white, silver, and clean sharp. He drove it into the chopping stump and turned back.

The birds made too much noise, a song neither amazing, nor of grace. He did not hear their song making him found, or sighted. Nor sweet was the sound. The birds were sparrows, worrisome and destructive, and though it was late in the season, a nest was not high off the ground in a cedar. The spatsies were low headed and shock-eyed. As he shook the tree the birds tumbled amazed and noisy. Two fought their wings and pin-wheeled into the high grass. The third, pink-chested and the runt, rolled head over around the trunk of the tree. Burley turned the bird over with a toe under its wing. The wing beat at the ground. Dust rose and covered the bird's eyes. Burley placed his bare foot on the bird's chest; he judged the heart faint, rapid and aviary. He stepped down. The feathers were soft. Blood bubbled at the bird's throat, erupted and quiet. The baby reeled once upon its wing and sucked at the air. Burley held the bird by its wing, faintly alive, still and sad. He threw the sparrow over the hog fence, heard the pitched, shrill surprise of the hog fight, sounding high, lonesome also, and without cause.

IN THE FALL OF THE YEAR HE TURNED TO HARVEST and it was not so bad. John Jr. made a fine worker, and even Nathan gave a true hand and when the corn came to sweet and swine feed. Harvest was fair, and for once without Breman standing on the other side of the last fence smiling and stomach-turning like purgative, Burley counted up his purse.

Jaretta Chapel was the most surprised when late in September Burley handed paint cans out of the wagon down to John Jr. and Nathan and Paul. She was even more surprised when she saw it was red barn paint. She had not planned to stay, having spread out her visits and worrying as the year moved. She was on the porch with Mattie and Priscilla fingering some new linen which she thought might make a good run of curtains. She saw the wagon and Burley and the cans, even came into the side yard and breathed over her Shem's shoulder into the bright ovals as the lids fell back.

"My God," she said. "If it's Christmas for sure I would have bought white paint for the house."

"Barn's needing first," Burley said, handing down another can. "Would you get back out of the way, Jaretta Chapel? I don't want the boys splashing none up on you."

Jaretta followed them out to the barn, even put her balance to one of the five-gallon cans, then gave her head one terrible twist to look at Burley high on a ladder throwing down brushes from the loft into her own hand.

"Catch," he said.

She threw the brush down. Burley did not see her again until the barn was painted.

Burley spent his chore up and down on the ladder, laying paint close and even under the eaves and in the hard-to-paint braces cantilevered over the cow pen. John Jr., Paul, and Nathan did most of the flat-board painting. Silas, only seven, spread his brush thin along the bottom sills, painting the tops of the weeds as he went. Burley did not chide him. Burley stood back and prided his work. Perhaps the paint was too red, the barn now too outrageous against the paintless house. He planned to paint the house white in the spring. There was some paint left over, so the smokehouse and the chicken shed were painted too—not all the chicken house. The paint went as far as the front door, one side facing the house, then trailed off, vanishing on the far side near the trees. The back never saw the paint, unless once Silas had carried his brush when he circled the shed running down a banty hen.

Burley and his sons slaughtered two hogs under the red eaves of the barn. The ground became redder as Burley slit the sows' throats, holding their heads high and without looking at the wild eyes, and let the pigs run, spilling silently down a rigged chute into the cow pen. Burley stood over the last fallen hog and walked the blood under his boots; his long apron dripped. By night, hams were wrapped and hung from the rafters above the slippery floor of the smokehouse. The remaining hog meat was packed down, bleeding and waiting tomorrow when he could separate the sides into bacon and put the rest away in salt. He came out of the shed blinking fast at the red sun. It was the middle of November. The sun was far down. A single lantern burned in the kitchen behind the shutters. Tomorrow would be cold.

He walked between the corn rows. The morning glories had withered and returned to the earth. He picked up a few stray ears, hard and pelletlike to throw over the fence to the cows. He had not cut the stalks in this field. The corn stretched away and planted on the hillside where he walked, the rows curved so he could not see clean to the far end of the field. He did not know he was running. The corn whipped and cut at his face. The corn was the shade of dun-colored breasts. He ran toward their milk, hurrying and running over footprints he remembered, and much smaller and more carefully placed, and lighter than his own, far and washed in the autumn rains. He could not have seen them. He blundered from the corn, veering across and tearing down stalks, into the last red line of the sun. The cobs crumbled in his fists, raining about his feet, mixing with tears as the giant eye winked and was gone.

HE EXPLAINED HIS VISIONS TO THE OLD WOMAN. THE Negress shifted her weight to the other side of her stool, put her hands wide, cracked, and lye-colored still, palm up on the table. The shutters were open, but in this season the light was cold and without color. It was afternoon, November, and he could not see her too well, sitting in the corner behind her table and the bottled waters. The white linen head rag floated above her featureless muddy face.

"You say they was like the udders of a cow," she said.

"I can't seem to sleep no more. You think because it's still her bed?"

"For sure you changed the sheets. All new, or the old ones washed and boiled in lye and water."

"Yes, I did," he said.

"Flopped the mattress over twice like I told you?"

"Yes, I did," he said.

Turning back when he left her, with no words ringing in his ears because she had given him no hope— just one thought when she pushed a copper-colored jar forward then brought it back into line, saying, "That won't do neither"—he looked back at Batina Nuntee with the shawl pulled tight at her throat against the wind. Because she had been at least kind he fetched her an armload of clean wood and laid it in a crate beside the hearth. She did not have a fire. When he was back on the horse she reached and laid her lye-colored hand on his boot in the stirrup. Her cold hand came through the leather. She said, "You can't clean the grates of a hot stove," and turned herself aside, retreating into the November afternoon, turning him out and away without hope or compensation, and under him the miles and bluffs back to his farm, and the red thumb of his own barn in the distance was visible through bare trees.

"Maybe I should have took her two armloads of

wood, Apples," he said to his mount. He had renamed the horse.

Vapor snakes coiled from the ponds and the stagnant winter course of the Salt River. Snow had fallen once, a trace which startled the eyes, and called the cows to moaning and was gone as the ground's heat took it. Clouds piled on the heights behind Batina Nuntee's. There would be snow again. It fell even before he was home. Paul was stacking wood against the kitchen door, filling the whole end of the porch. Mattie would not have to call the boys out of their laziness for at least a month. Probably into Christmas as she tried her hand at Christmas pies.

Christmas came; Burley was unprepared for it. Before, Daliah's emotional hands had made the holidays. He took little notice until the day came. He did slide through the woods with Paul, John Jr., Nathan, and Silas even, to find a lone spruce in the side of a varve thrown on the shore of Long Pond. His axe rang out three times into the granite air, spinning the doomed pine from its roots and silently over into the snow. Burley rubbed his ungloved hands. He told Silas to carry his axe. John Jr. carried the tree at its severed end. Paul was in the middle, lost and small in the branches. Nathan kept the spire off the ground.

Burley made a few surprises. Burgess was the most vocal about the gold star. Burley swung him in his own proud reach for Burgess to render the star.

"Best star out of heaven," Burgess said.

"Best star out of Boetiger's leastways," Jaretta said. Jaretta Chapel and her three children, Shem and Mathew and Priscilla, were over for trimming the tree. "You have been free with money this season," she said.

"I only bought the star," Burley said.

"What about these oranges?" She handled one from the bowl on the table, turned it over and around. "A dozen oranges don't come without price. By God, these come from Florida, John!" She had taken to calling him John in front of the children.

"Dali always saw they had something."

Jaretta sat beside him at the fire. She moved a hand on his shoulder. Burley did not mind anymore. "You've accepted she's gone."

He threw another log on the fire, sent the flame sputtering around green wood. The fire dimmed before it caught. Out of the darkness the star shone. "I've accepted that she isn't here for now," he said.

"Has to be more, John." Jaretta tried her other hand on his shoulder again. He moved from under it; threw another log on. It was not needed. He poked at the coals.

Jaretta spoke low against the children hearing in a far corner. "Once before you were married, my sister Beth and I fetched her for a choir practice." Jaretta pulled the hem of her skirt back above her shoes and put her feet on the warm brick. "We came down between them bare maples and she was on the porch in that coat of her brother's and them near summer shoes, not even sheltering behind the dry vines where the wind was at least cut, and not in the house. But then, we knew her father. She came down into the snow, leaving deep prints about her bare ankles. I moved over and brought her under the blankets. Her hands were red, and oh so cold. I held them all the way to church." Jaretta shifted her feet back from the fire. "The choir sang 'Leaning on the Everlasting Arms.' I never heard Daliah Faye sing better."

"You don't know she won't be back," Burley said.

"I can't count on it. I can't count that our choir

will ever hear her voice again. To hear her sweet song. I sorely this Christmas would buy her the highest pair of fur boots I could lay money down on," Jaretta said, without hands anywhere near Burley's frame. "Poke at that fire some more. Christmas don't have to be so cold."

THE MORNING WAS LIME; THE AIR WAS HEAVY, QUICK, white, and caustic cold. He threw open the single great shutter, threw his man-smell like a stale breath, or corn whiskey in sour water, or an untouched air absent many months of woman flesh and any cloth approaching silk, against the biting and yet quiet cold. Outside his bedroom window the pale new year grew crystalline just before sunrise, brightened and tucked the steadfast shadows under the crawl space of the outbuildings, under the tree limbs and in their forks, and far away to the dark line of the river. Under the side wall of the red barn the color was maroon as dried blood. He waited at the window five minutes, counting back: January, December, November . . . ten months almost. He came down off the porch stamping into the hard winter boots. They were his hunting boots, well soaped against the rot of the cold. It was his obligation. The air was worse as he moved. Transparent ice sheets shattered into knives as he broke through them, stabbing his lungs painfully and suffocatingly. He headed for the barn, passed it by, and in the tool shed found his twenty-pound sledge little used and rusted. Cows moaned around the pond, came close and nudged his side as he edged onto the ice. He lifted the hammer. It came down on the ice.

Damn cows. Sell every one of them. The hammer came down again. Rebound carried it higher. One great-faced cow came out onto the ice behind him, terrified and impatient to drink. *Live off hog meat.* His hands were cold. He had forgotten his gloves again. His breath was in the air a white storm, labored and pained, and just as impatient. *Hog meat!* The ice cracked. *Bacon. Ham.*

Lost in his breath-fog, cows came up against his side, splay-legged and falling as the ice gave way beneath them. His hammer-rings echoed and flurried among the bare trees. The cold was over his boots, rode the trough behind his knees, behind his cold thighs, iced loins, fine hard breathing chest. The upturned cow legs picketed in front of his hairless face and he was drowning in her face red as bourbon over cracked ice and a frost-laced hand rag was against his lips; and the gray hands of gods cast down the lintels of his doors, threw them down in Jericho amid the chords of an old song she sang for him: "That saved a wretch like me"—words frozen and impaled on the cornstalks he made heave from the ground into the lockjawed leer of Breman who yelled across the fence Burley's secrets at her. He wanted to tell Daliah himself, to shut out Breman's face, though it did not matter; she could not hear either of them. She still sang: "I once was lost, but now I'm found" through her cold teeth framed by her loosened, never-braided hair held above her ears by combs of ice. The cows came around again, tearing the sheet ice with grinding forelegs as the animals crashed onto the bank. Ice already formed on their hides. Burley rose forward like a berg, righted and was on the bank too, ice-covered beneath the legs of steers.

He must have lain many minutes in the wind. The hammer no longer echoed, though he wished it did; he hated to think he could lay frozen longer than a hammer-ring. He thought he heard the screen door open. The house was not that far away. He heard it close. *Paul'll have to be needing a lot more wood to come this far up the lot.* He waited to hear the wood chop. *Naw, he would have had enough last night. Mattie could have burned much. Only Dali would of . . .*

Feet came in front of him. He turned his head. John Jr. said, "Pa, you all right?"

"I'm cold," he said.

They stripped him of his clothes, standing him before the fire as the frozen cloth broke with his skin. Mattie made him tea. He did not like it. There was soup too. They had a time with his boots. John Jr. worked one, Nathan the other, turning his heels and ankles until the leather gave and his matted socks came away too. His sons rubbed his feet. Before they lay him in bed he saw Burgess at the fire, dimly etched, beating at the frozen boots with the wooden mallet from his Christmas toy.

HE HAD A FEVER FOR THREE DAYS, PNEUMONIA FOR THE rest of January, and weeks into February. He missed the worst of the snows. They told him the drifts were near seven feet in places. Mattie and Carlene placed a spoon against his blue lips and waited for him to swallow. He watched them with cold eyes. Mattie said he looked better; he did not believe her. Even Jaretta spooned for him once. She talked easily of the choir, and the church, and the snow, little at all about his accident and illness, as if to talk about it was to admit he was sick, and once she admitted it she would have to feign compassion for John Burley Mead, and therefore would have to stop coming over to see him in his sickbed. Even his sons came and stopped at his bedside and told him how they were carrying on. His few head of cattle they had

[121]

turned loose above the barn into the hills to forage. Nathan and Paul said they would round them up at spring thaw.

Snow remained on the ground forty-three days.

By March he needed to be out. He placed his feet under him for one quick trip to the barn. He did not glance toward the pond and the broken ice thrown up and this late gorged about the banks. He walked straight to the barn, took one full turn among the hay feeds, smelled the ripe and mildew stench. He did not make the trip down to the barn again for two weeks.

And it was the middle of March. The last of the hog meat was coming down out of the smokehouse. They lived now on ham hock and dried shell peas from the corn rows. He tasted little of them. The children did not complain. Mattie made cakes to keep the little ones quiet. At the end of the month, the ground thawed again, he was in the tack shed readying and repairing harness for the coming season. Much of the leather was mildewed and sadly cracked. The hame lines at best were rotted. He had forgotten to tell his sons to keep up with the tack.

He did not mark the anniversary when it returned. He was already into the spring plowing, working the kitchen garden outside the back door. It was April again. He saw the carriage pass the boundary of the gatepost, saw the violent wheel wrenching speed as the ruts new returned after the winter snow gave way to the spinning spokes. Jaretta was down fast out of the carriage, spilling out of the bright paint into the roadway.

Burley was whittling stakes for the garden, new limber willow trelliswork and beanpoles. His knife did not cease to pile shavings at his feet even as Jaretta Chapel was down in his face, speaking and making no sense at all.

". . . it's right in my hand, John," she said.

"Was there postage due, or what?" he said.

"Boetiger handed it to me right through the cage. I almost died when I saw the handwriting!"

He took the letter in his hand.

"She's alive," she said.

"This post says Ona, Florida," he said, rising and already making for the barn and the once-ridden horse.

"You didn't even read it," Jaretta called after the running mare. She ran along the fence, cut across the yard, and headed Burley off before he made the turn onto the County Line Road beside the white-railed cemetery fence. He came face to face with one of the markers; it was Brett's, he almost stumbled over it as his horse righted and carried into the east and Harrodsburg. "You should have read the letter!" she yelled.

CHAPTER FIVE

NOVEMBER

1963

SAMUEL STILL HAD THE BROOM IN HIS HAND COMING into the kitchen. He had swept the walk after Dison Jane had come inside, quitting the afternoon and the bulbs. She was now in the back room beside the refrigerator sewing quilts, flawed because her eyes failed, and the color was unwise: green against pink, against maroon flowers.

Samuel moved to another window, following fast about the kitchen, even moving to the back room where Dison Jane sewed. She did not look up when he came in. She did not stop.

"Nothing," he said.

"Then why are you watching him?" she said.

"It's just that yellow hat." Samuel laid a hand on the glass. He wiped away his breath-fog. "It looks like one of your dried apple pies on his head."

"He wanted a red one. You believe what he would have looked like with a red one!"

Otho was in the garage only minutes. He passed where apples once dried in halves and quarters and eighths on quilting frames over fruit stands stenciled in heavy letters, passed the toolshed that held rusted saws and lathes, and green copper nails in sealed jars, hunting knives dull under years, abandoned twines, ropes and hemps, battered boxes, and brown mason jars in bushel baskets. The padlock hung open in the hook so that the wind blew the door, beat a tattoo on the wood frame, letting in the wind and wet through the small unpaned window.

"What was that you say?" he said. "I mean what was that you were saying?"

"I catch him turning small things over in his hands, odd buttons, and fish weights, and empty gun shells."

"Toys," he said.

Dison Jane pulled the thread tight in short jerks bringing her hand over her head. "Buttons, weights, shells." She said, "You think I should use this green wool here?"

"It's blue."

"What?"

"It's blue. Not green," he said, turning from the window, just a second blind. Otho moved by his window. Samuel had mistimed him. Otho did not look up at the window. Samuel stepped back anyways.

"Why didn't you say he wasn't wearing his coat?" Dison Jane said. "Damn the yellow hat! You didn't say he wasn't wearing his coat."

———

Seldom-worn serge and bitter-melt calico prints, unstructured Sunday suits, and on a shelf above, two hats (one unblocked, the other without veil) reposed in gray shades and a negative once-white reek of a woman's talcum perspired into icings and the perfume of sweatsalt and sawdust. Otho's coat was on an inside hook. Samuel moved aside boxes, most of them empty and light, airless bubbled egg cartons and tennis shoe boxes. Stacks of church literature were tied in twines. Ivory soap bars anesthetized white linens. In a lacquered frame a full portrait of a girl, Great-Aunt Carlene, faded in beige against a background of a house and five wooden steps. A large brooch that looked like yellow glass rested on her breast. Her face was round above a roped neck, unpainted like plain porcelain. The frame was over-large; there was no room about the walls. Instead hundreds of photographs gathered Dison's and Otho's six children and the six children's twenty-three sons and daughters. Months of newspapers rotted in twine. Boxes upon boxes remained empty, and boxes fitted together with other smaller boxes inside like Chinese puzzles. Unrelated figurines populated mantels. Christ looked down from calendars and postcards, Sunday school pamphlets and three crucifixes. A thousand people flooded the room, thronging and splashing about his ears.

"Why did you let her talk you out of the red hat?" Samuel said.

"I just went out to the car shed to fetch some things."

"This coat's got pockets big enough for fruit jars." Samuel handed it to him. "You could fetch a day's worth of buttons, weights, and shells and make one trip of it."

"You can't wear a red hat to church. By God, I wear a yellow hat. I'm not ashamed to be seen by a fish that ain't Baptist or even Episcopal. I take out the hooks when I go to church."

"She didn't make me get the coat."

"Dison's not Episcopal either."

"I would have bought the red hat."

"They was three dollars apiece. I couldn't buy a brown and a red one." Otho traced the crown. "I got her to settle on the yellow."

Samuel thought a moment. "She doesn't settle easy, does she?"

"In forty-nine years she did it twice," Otho said. "This yellow hat . . . and letting me tell you about Daliah Faye."

"She probably wishes she had left you on your own in the hat store with them extra dollars to spend."

Otho shook his hand underneath the coat. He laughed. "What makes you think I didn't have to pay her three dollars this morning just to let you in the door."

"Because she would have give me them three dollars not to listen to you," Samuel said, "and I only got thirty-five cents in my pockets."

"Thirty-five cents wouldn't buy much."

"I'd pay thirty-five cents just to hear you say Daliah Faye Brownlee."

Otho leaned forward. No lights burned in the room, and a film of November settled over the chairs and layered like a grainy mist under his hands. "Of my grandbabies I know you are the one," he said quietly and unashamed, coming too close and giving secrets. "I have seen your eyes when the picture box comes out while the others craved cartoon books." He pulled the pistol out of the fumbling coat. "I got her used to the fish weights and buttons, then I got the gun shells. I was working up to bringing out this gun. It's a Starr Army double-action six shot. Your Great-Great-Grandpa Brownlee carried it in his war."

"It's heavy," Samuel said.

"I thought so too, the first time."

"Will it fire?"

"I fired it but once. But Daddy never took it from the canned goods shelf to work it out. You see"—he rocked forward—"it's took some abuse. Was even some rust before I cleaned it. I used light utility oil after that. It won't shine, but it won't rust neither." Otho rocked back. "Even if it is a hundred years old this day."

"You say Mr. Brownlee fired this gun?"

"Rensselaer Brownlee for sure. His sons maybe. My daddy might of. I did for sure—the last time too. Summer of 1904 to my mind was the last time."

"You have that memory for sure?"

"Sure. The gun ain't been out of my possessing since," Otho chuckled. "Daddy had to let me have it. As such I almost killed with it."

"You killed a man?" Samuel asked.

"You got to know Daddy was powerful given to the gun." Otho took the revolver back. He traced the barrel, sighted along it, and did not pull the trigger. "I was thirteen that summer and I recall that Burgess was seventeen and mean. What I say is, Burgy was made rakish, a hellion as far as Mama was said. But Daddy would not call him on it, like any understanding between a man and his son was full-blown between the two. So I guess that's why Burgess told me to get the gun for him. He alone could have asked Daddy, who would not have refused him. But he had to affront the understanding by asking me to do his stealing of Daddy's gun. Daddy could not love me." Otho said it flat, like it was an admission, that if fault was his, he shouldered it all. "When Daddy caught it missing he went right up to Burgess. Burgess told him the truth. Truth was what Burgy called convenience. And I saw them both on the porch, right there under starlight, and Burgess's wild white teeth flashed in the pale, until Daddy shook him and I was near thirteen, and mad at Burgess and hating Daddy for a second where I was under that pear tree already rotting because it was August and hot. Hating him loving Burgy so much that Burgy could tell him the truth and not help me to the loving. And Daddy not loving me as I found out later because I was his bastard baby. I shot the gun right over his head. I said to Daddy

[131]

I was aiming at Burgess. Daddy's hair was covered with the wood splinters from the eaves where the bullet hit, it was so close. He said to me, 'How determined are you to kill him?' and I said, 'Just enough to move up in his place and see more than your hand on his shoulder from behind.' I said I was only thirteen and already mad at them both. And Daddy said, 'Well, now. Well, now. Seems I got no more claim on that pistol. I thought it was her hand to be next pulling, but I find it is her hand give to me without choice. I best let you keep it by proxy. Just you ask her when I should turn my back next for her. And remember it is her pappy's gun. I was just her holster for a while.' And as he walked away I said to him, 'Daddy, I don't want Burgy sleeping in my bed tonight.' And he looked back over his shoulder, his neck straining and veined under starlight, and I knew he agreed with me. 'Burgy? He'd be ashamed to have you at his side. Now that he knows I trust you more than I do him.' "

So that's it. So that's it, Samuel thought.

Otho rolled the chambers, and rotating behind his thumb, spun empty fortune.

CHAPTER SIX

APRIL

1893

SHE HAD ALREADY WALKED THE KITCHEN TWICE, not walked around but through from the doorway, by the table and its sheltering chairs, to the window where she saw the red barn. She turned back, the baby and the satchel on opposite hips, as if to turn and speak to Jaretta waiting breathlessly in the silver breezeway, but turned back and paced the straight path through and looked at the red paint again.

"Why didn't he paint the house first, Jaretta?" she asked. "Couldn't you have steered his brush over to these house walls?"

"You got that child bundled too tight, like he was potatoes in a sack," Jaretta said.

"He's already had one cold," Daliah said.

Jaretta steadied herself with a hand on the table. Daliah had turned on her, dismissing the red barn. Jaretta said, "John isn't here."

Daliah blinked once, twice. "Has he rode to Judge Randall for the divorce because of this child?"

"Dali," Jaretta said. "He doesn't know about this baby." She steadied her other hand, leaning far out over the table, laying her words carefully, supported like silverware on the surface. "He never read the letter. He could be riding that horse to Florida. How many days you figure it would take for him to turn around and

[135]

head back before he figured you might not be worth the trip?"

"Him?"

"Four days he went into Indiana," Jaretta said.

"Why Indiana?—oh, Bea," she said.

Daliah placed her satchel down, let the faded roses bloom, wither, and decay in upon themselves, crumble as in a vacuum around her new dresses, stays crisp and confining, and one singular pair of patent leather shoes. With one hand empty, she wanted to take off her gloves.

Jaretta said, "Here," and took the child.

Daliah removed her gloves slowly. She took them off a joint at a time, alternating fingers and starting again on the other hand. She had watched the ladies in Tampa. That was how they removed their gloves.

"This child doesn't have much weight," Jaretta said. "You wean him on oranges, or what?"

Daliah laid her gloves out like pale hands on the table. "Burley been gone long?"

"Yesterday afternoon—early." Jaretta jiggled the child, brought the baby upward to feel his breath on her cheek. "You don't understand yet, do you? Burley rides out after you, not against you. I've watched him this past year—this year you saw fit to steal out of your husband's and your children's lives."

Daliah started to protest; her eyes narrowed and grew quiet, distant. The room and her child and Jaretta Chapel danced a bright step in the April light.

"Now I says, I have seen this man Burley." Jaretta cuddled the baby below her left arm. The child passed a bubble in the corner of his mouth. Jaretta pressed it away with her thumb. "I tried to fault him, tried to shame him to surrender his pride, to admit he erred you, cheated you." Jaretta shifted the baby. "He's wet," she said.

Daliah folded the diaper once, then over again. She had taken off her hat, thrown aside the gauze construction as she had thrown aside the satchel's roses. She fastened the pin and was drawing the shirt over the child's legs when she turned back on Jaretta and said, "You can't deny he gave little comfort in these walls he built. Neither me nor the children had of him what we didn't come to take. We ate; we survived; we did not prosper."

"You rant as if this Florida was paved with gold!"

"Who says it isn't?"

"Could just be orange peels," Jaretta said.

Daliah threw clothing out of her baggage: a green dress, pale embroidered chemise which Jaretta fingered closely and laid back on the table.

"Who says it isn't?" Daliah asked again.

"Then why did you come back? This man you bedded with . . ." Jaretta controlled her words. "I must say, this man that kept you, slept you, gave you a year of taffeta silk, parasols, and my God!" she said, picking them up, "the finest pair of white kid gloves I ever saw— I could be jealous of you!—why did you come back?"

"He wanted my baby," Daliah said.

Jaretta smiled.

"Cass's eyes are blue."

Jaretta fumbled in her apron. "Shoot. I forgot I gave the letter to John. But that's what you meant by green-eyed chances. I didn't stop to think anyone of us might be color-blind."

Daliah laughed. "Maybe Burl thought he *was* painting the barn white!"

"He is going to paint the house, you know," Jaretta said. "I've seen the order down at Boetiger's. Paint's to be in the first of May."

The baby was on the table between them, rolling

his head from side to side with unfocused green eyes. A small bubble was again at the corner of his mouth. It broke.

"There never"—Daliah laughed—"I mean there *never* was a green-eyed person in my family!"

"We shouldn't." Jaretta stifled her laughter, put her hands high on her flushed cheeks. "We must be serious."

"Why?" Daliah said, coming down. "Why, so I can rearrange and pack on my wifely chores again? I have to start as it was again?"

"Then I ask you again. Why did you come back?" Jaretta laid a hand over Daliah's, her forearm was across the baby. He kicked her arm twice.

Daliah drew away. "I had to come back."

She was at the window again, stabbing out at the brave April light as if her fingers were knives, jabbing and cursing the red paint. It was not yet late in the day. Her children were not yet out of school, had not yet placed their feet on the County Road where she had made them walk in her mind's eye during her winter in Florida. The road had not yet taken up her husband and his horse because not knowing where he was, she had not imagined his travel. Carlene had always been quiet (perhaps God had given and taken much in the unweaving of Brett from her), and Burgess, now four years old, independent, and without loneliness, was about in quiet play—like his father. There was the barn. The red barn.

Daliah's fingers stabbed back into the room, about the cane-bottomed chairs, the sideboard, the rugless oak floor. Jaretta for once was a wan ghost among the room's markers. "Resewing and seaming cut down clothes for my children until there's not a button what matches on a shirt. Eating fat cuts of pork in March as we come out of winter. Nickel cans of sardines. Sturdy shoes, lye soap, and hame string pulls on the shutters!"

"You are thirty-three years old, Dali," Jaretta said. The baby was fighting sleep. "How long before you are resigned? The boys have their father. He's taught them to be men—albeit, men like himself. But how can we change men? You and me, Dali, we take them in, care for them, feed them greens in season, and now and then place a banana cake in front of them to remind them it's their birthday, and mend their shirts with only white thread, and smile once and have them breed sons just like them, such is a man. But you have girls. Carlene's not old enough yet to cry because she is only a woman. She can't be made to stand up to them yet the way you and I—and now your own Mattie." Jaretta could have cursed Daliah, the curse laying on her tongue unsaid because she did not blaspheme those she loved. "Your poor Mattie has come into her own this year. If I were you I'd fall at her feet and cry in a fashion that would shame God himself."

"I said I would make it up to her, Jaretta." Daliah quieted herself. She caught her breath, placed air quick and humble under her breast. "She is my best—Mattie."

"Then why do we curse them being children?" Jaretta said.

"How else can we curse them to grow up like us?" Daliah said.

Daliah and Jaretta walked with hands around each other's waists like girls passing secrets, though they did not speak again. Jaretta did not say farewell as she leaned far out from under the covered carriage. Daliah was up on the porch. The afternoon sun faced her square, backlighting the spokes of the buggy as the wheels passed the gates. Under the white blooms of the pear tree, Jaretta's beautiful face floated back at Daliah, quiet, adjusted and without fear now that best friends were again best friends. The barn was red, but she dismissed it now, having already raged and put it past. The dust of the yard was raked in half-circles. The splayed mimosa fronds waved rhythmically like river weeds. The fences were lined with horsetail, the cemetery markers were shrouded in jimson and chickweed. She did not need to see them. She could recite the words from memory. In strong light the ghosts did not stand. The fieldstone walls of the well. Cows on a hill. Chickens.

Burgess and Carlene came out of the barn, hand in hand. She wanted to turn from the porch, but was rooted. Their arms swung. Burgess's hair was cut round and was wind-blown forward. Carlene's hair was pulled back severely behind her ears. Their faces were pink.

Burgess said, "Carly says we got to see this 'ere baby doll."

———————

HER SONS CROWDED IN A HALF-CIRCLE AROUND THE BABY. Her children came forward to see, except Mattie, who hung back from the others, with her high face unlined and unfair. Daliah watched her over the heads of her sons. *That's all right*, she thought. *Give it out easy, explain it to her, what you owe.*

John Jr. said, "Daddy never said."

Of course he never said. He don't even know. Daliah began, "Your father always prided himself on sons," and spoke more loudly, right over to Mattie. "No matter how different you was. No matter how you came to him."

Mattie came up through the boys, moved Paul and Nathan away from the table. She did not look down at

[140]

the baby. She looked into Daliah's face. She said, "Daddy's got a number of months of pride to catch up on, looks to me."

Daliah would not hedge. "And some months of false pride to overlook," she said. "—looks to me."

Daliah brought down the dishes from the shelf. The wares were still familiar: the cracked platter bowls, the ecru serving vessel. She remembered the favorites, placing Burgess's blue bowl at his father's right hand. She left Burley's setting empty. She turned away. Mattie came behind her and put a white plate at Burley's chair.

"And when the baby was four months old I could travel with him. It was a long trip, longer than the going," Daliah said.

"How could it have been longer? You packed your bag three weeks before you left. Yes, I knew. It was spring then. We do clean to the floor in spring."

Daliah turned quickly, a dull spoon in her hand, poking it in Mattie's face. She saw the plate where Mattie had set it. "Why didn't you tell him?"

"You were still my mother then." Mattie put down another setting. "You stopped being my mother. Just in fall, when he came out of the house running barefoot in the cold morning—you know how his lungs hurt him at times—and thought I was you out cutting wood to get up biscuits for breakfast." Mattie put down the remaining plates, put it all down, and gave out. "I found him crying in the corn in November. Christmas he cut a tree without his gloves and I cried that time because his hands were so red. In January he fell through the ice at the pond and was in bed a month. By then there were no more chickens. Nathan found the last three frozen on their nests. So I made him a broth of hog fat and barley and fed him. He called me Daliah twice." Mattie walked over to the stove and stirred at a pan. Daliah had not

moved. "And then I, too, almost thought I was you."
She stopped stirring.

Daliah stirred a pan too. She stood beside Mattie at
the stove. Each had a pot. Neither needed to be stirred.

"Was he bad sick, his lungs?" Daliah asked.

Mattie raised her spoon. She tasted the soup, added
nothing. She stirred some more. "I don't know. Daddy
never says much to me. He keeps his secrets to himself
or for the boys. I'm just a girl."

Daliah could not reply immediately to that, then
sorting and tumbling the jumble in her mind, she spoke
it out.

"The day you was born, your daddy was sleeping in
the breezeway. Jaretta Chapel was over to see me because I was sixteen and I was scared. I was laying on my
back fighting off the pains, hoping the hurting would go
because if I woke Jaretta she would wake Burley and
then the pain would have to be real." Daliah laid aside
her spoon. Stirring confused her thinking. She needed
the memory clean and precise. "I think I knew you
aimed coming to me a girl. I didn't want to disappoint
your daddy. No woman in her first childbed wants the
child wrong given to her man's likes. Sons were what he
needed. Eighty acres to work, and there was Jaretta—I
could see them through the crack of the door when she
left it open—kicking Burley in the side, saying: 'Go get
the doctor.' He rose up fast, cold air on his back, stamping into his boots. He was upon the mule." Daliah
placed her hand on the spoon. She did not pick it up
again, only fingered the wood handle, gripping like
hands in labor. "I was relieved quickly. When he was
gone I knew I could have you fast, not mattering if you
was a girl. He was gone for the doctor and if I could
have you on my own without their man's help I could
keep you safe to myself. He would have no claim on

you. You was my girl baby, and who needs many sons to measure when they have a baby girl?"

Daliah looked back for Mattie. She was behind Burley's place at the table, with her hands on his plate. Mattie cradled his plate softly, returned it to the shelf, and was gone out the breezeway door.

THE LINEN SOFTNESS BETRAYED HER AND HER BED; WHERE in a year she had been lulled by down bedding, the crackling of the husk called her home more than the dustless April mile she had walked from the railroad. The air was dark and the growing April moon focused on her window and lay across her fertile and spent womb. She memoried how the moon had stolen a few square yards beside the bed, lighted it, and had crept with the pale linen glow up the opposite wall. The moon called her from sleep, forced remembering of early in her marriage like ignited flash powder frozen and captured—the very moment when the moonlight had lain across his body, highlighting him from his loins to his dark head. Something in the air came down, collapsed upon itself like the satchel, leaving in the air numbered minutes, flashing over seconds and never-taken sepia photographs—if there might have been a camera box to record them—the seventeen (minus one) years she and Burley had bartered between them and put away in an album. A photograph fell and she was in the choir again, singing "Shall We Gather at the River"; looking down from the raised perch of the choir loft into the young man's upturned face, his hands laid flat on the unopened hymnal. And another explosion of flash powder blew into the air and settled down into the dust motes suspended in the late afternoon sunlight

[143]

when Batina Nuntee spread hands and gave her twins.

She gave up images freely—people's faces: Jaretta Chapel above her in the morning heat when Mattie came to her, speaking (though she could not hear), and for a moment she swore Jaretta Chapel breathed life into her child's lungs and made her cry; Mattie, too, her girl baby coming down off the lost years when the children came too fast, bore out of her and grew faster than she could turn around and see them pass her as she stooped to help the next one up: until there was Brett and Carlene, and she did not care to see them grow, settling into her fastness and milk-colored sheets; small Burgess's face was unformed—his four years (minus one) were trapped like a blurred image in the photo shutter.

A new face formed: she was unsure of it also, seeing it inverted and measured on wet, undeveloped plates, finally swimming upward in the solution. She thought it was her father; there was the same proportion, but unstooped, the same eyes but unclouded; those blue china eyes of Caslin's, leaning at the mantel unsure and without accusation. She did not have the satchel under the bed. It was packed and in the closet. He would not have looked there.

"I promise," she lied.

His hand slid down the door facing. His face was framed by the late March beyond the open door. The parquet floor was in place (except for a few new cut and slightly miscolored pieces; the workman had not found all the woodwork she had thrown through the door) and was waxed and now perfect and hopeful. Outside his carriage waited. The air was warm, ripe like wet dust, a watermelon air.

"Promises and curses." He started to close the door. Pinin held the horse and was within hearing. Caslin did not care. He spoke naturally and without caution. "So I promise I will see you to the train. I will lift your baggage up myself. And tip the porter to guarantee your safety." His hand moved up the facing, pushing the door open. His hand was level with her eyes, the fingers curved around the thickness of the frame, well manicured, amateur, and not long disciplined to any work unbacked by his wealth. For a brief moment she pitied his hands, and would suffer them her calluses to tell him what she desired.

"You needn't pay the train Negro for my passage. I can take care of myself."

"I have to pay him. I should pin a tag to your breast like a child sent to relatives. Nothing as simple as name and town and Please-Be-Kind-To-This-Child." Caslin broadened his words. "I should write: Shipper incurs no liability. She is free on board by her own making."

"I said I would wait until you return. I can give you three days—until April," she said.

The door was fully open now. He was no longer supported by the dark wood. He stood before the bright green of the front lawns. He looked back at her from the first step below the porch.

"Three days I'll be gone," he said. "Can't you wait three days?"

"I promise," she lied again.

She watched the carriage come around in the drive. Before she closed the door she saw Caslin sitting back under the shade of the hood, his unworked hands fisted around the reins, and his left foot propped against the dash, bound in brass leather and brilliant in the sun. She looked away, into the new booming face of the clock in the foyer. She shut the door and hurried to her room, bringing out the rose-colored satchel, well packed. From the new windows, set almost square in place of the former dormer (and the dress dummy and its candy-tin letters), she memoried the spinning turn of his yellow spokes flashing, the sand popping . . .

. . . popping grainy clouds of her photograph memory thinned. She was a large album, and laying in her bed her eyes could not close beneath the bare ceiling slope. She twisted her head. The starlight was soft, the linens textured in light like cotton wadding. The baby was swaddled beside her, had been asleep since she had placed him so. He was a tight oval in the angle between her arm and side. She closed her elbow, testing the surety of his size. The linen further from them grew misshapen and empty under the soft moon. *No supposing the carpetbag would last another trip.* She twisted her head back. She almost reached for the baby, to wake him and see his green eyes black in the dark and satisfy her own righteousness. Instead she rose from the bed, looking back over the curve of sheets which was her son under moon, and took the door quietly. The evening air assaulted her. The breezeway was silver, and noiselessly she listened at the other doors for her breathing children. At Mattie's and Carlene's door she heard a bedspring complain. She would not speak to her now. Leaning against the porch post, she sang softly "As Pants the Hart for Cooling Streams"; she sighed, and cried a little while the white flowers drifted down against the uncountable stars. Pale colors rose, and the odor was of locust blooms crushed beneath wheels, beneath a cat's paw.

———

"YOU GOT TO PUT THE SEAMS TOGETHER LIKE THEY WAS the joints of a stovepipe," Daliah said to Mattie.

[146]

"Like this," Mattie said.

Morning was bright over the locust trees, shining full and warm into the clearing beside the house between the smoke shed and the path down to the chicken roost. Quilting frames were in place and Daliah and Mattie worked the new muslins in the sun. The baby slept in the hammock-shaped hollow of one of the frames; he stirred now and then, and Daliah watched him closely. She reasoned the sun would be good for him. She planned to wean him from the warmth, to have him accustomed for winter when it came again.

"He weighed near seven and a half pounds I'd imagine. Not the biggest. Silas was a good nine!"

Mattie threw a completed sheet across the wire fence. There was now a row of them begun, not near what Daliah would have started by this time of year. Mattie had not kept up with the mending. Some were sewn and resewn. Others were new and harsh, unblanched by the night dews.

"Mama," Mattie said. "This man? Was he handsome? I mean, was that what made you give him a year, living, and—" Mattie stopped.

Daliah folded a sheet over, folded it over again onto its creases, and put it on the pile with others. The locust blooms looked like crushed pearls in the morning light. A cat crossed the yard, yellow striped and thin. It pressed around her ankles, bristling and rubbing. Its fur was matted and scratched her legs.

"Handsome is of no depth; he was fair and well tanned. His eyes were handsome, pale blue like sun-dried asters." Daliah fingered the cloth near at hand, musing, and safe because she recalled, and that was relief. "If he was riding the fields he would come back all one color, not a shade one would call dust. It was like newspaper, a flat color like he was printed on the back-

[147]

ground of rust-edged grass and cane." Daliah frowned, she had struck something, a chord that would justify, but then she dismissed it. "The man had no sides," she said.

"Did you love him?"

"I desired him," Daliah said. "Now desire is what you must know. You have turned your head after church when you fancied a young man?"

Mattie blushed. "Yes, Mama."

"Some more than that, I say, not just a foolish heart like a girl's hope, flattering and vain. I am thirty-three years old. I am not beautiful anymore. I did not desire fretting my vanity against his smooth leather and chintz spreads." Daliah stepped away from the cat. "Yes, he is handsome. Handsome in his surroundings, handsome in his attitude." She smiled for Mattie. "I desired him."

"Over Daddy?"

"As was early on with your daddy. Where did this cat come from?" Daliah shoved the animal with her foot. The cat rubbed against her again.

"Burgy found him in the road. A stray."

Daliah looked under the blowing corner of the muslin at the cat, square and lined under the shade of the sheeting. "Burgess is a stray himself."

"Is that why you fault him—and Daddy? Because they are strays?" Mattie gathered an armload of the linens. "But you are right. They are strays. What else can they be when you do not love them."

Daliah stopped in the middle of a fold. When she looked up Mattie was already halfway across the yard. The sheets were piled above her head, brilliant in the white of the sun.

Daliah worked at the material another quarter hour. She was too shamed to move; her legs could not be trusted to carry her to the house. Besides Mattie was there, and facing her was worse than sweating in the

sun. The muslin wire fence steadied her hand. A stray
cow came abreast of its mesh and turned back moaning;
Burgess, chasing the june bug drift, stumbled at the
fence and the shrill insect faded; rank weeds like hen
feathers were pinned to chicken wire by the wind. She
circled the cemetery twice before the fence would let
her go. A path was trod straight from the gate to the
porch, and as she stepped up, she dropped the armload
of muslin, which cascaded in ropes about her feet. She
turned because she had forgotten her baby under the
sun. She turned; she saw him.

HE SAW HER DRAPED IN THE CLOTH. HE HAD SEEN THE
woman's figure from the hilltop, as he jogged fired and
unfilled upon his horse. As he topped the bluff above
the river, the tin barn roof rang like a silver point. She
could have been Mattie, at least Jaretta Chapel. He had
not hurried down into the wild spring mustard to re-
claim a familiar face. Though he should have known.
Should have been prepared.

"How could you—"

She cut him off. "I have entered no contest at
which you are the judge." Her face was perfectly blank.
"Jaretta told me you didn't read the letter. She drove
over, you could have found courtesy to read my explanation."

"You are standing on the sheets," he said. The
horse stepped forward. He stepped her back. "Mattie
might not favor disturbing her hand work."

"I sewed this one myself," she said.

"You remember how, do you?" He looked over her.
She wore a plain but new green dress. "Them clothes
don't look like your handcraft."

[149]

"Store-bought." She lifted her skirt.

"Cash money?"

She dropped her pleats, smoothed them nervously. "I said, you could at least have read the letter. You never had no sympathy for my desires."

"Nor you for my plans," he said.

"You think this is an apology?" She faced him square; sitting his horse and with her five steps up on the porch, their faces were level. "You can't know what I'll have to apologize for. Why don't you guess?"

He thought quickly, but thinking tumbled and nothing would stick. She was attractive and that startled him. She had changed and change was foreign to him. Her hair was not even in combs, was down about her shoulders and he was surprised to see how long it was still. Her face was pale and unflawed. He wanted to shock her. "I cleared one-twelve-fifty-three after taxes," he said. "I painted the barn red." His face was smug.

She said quickly, "I had another baby," and turned away.

He spurred the horse roughly, reining her toward the barn. "Damn her!" he said. *Looks as if I bought me a hundred and twelve dollar and fifty-three cent bastard baby!*

MATTIE WAS THE FIRST TO TRY HIM. SHE CAME TO HIM just before noon, flowing with her easy youth into the cool barn where he had been sitting the past half hour. He watched her come quickly, stepping high over the ruts, the cow droppings, the snake mounds, framed by the open door and the April white surrounding her fresh, and dew crisp.

She said, "Daddy, what are you going to do?"

"You choosing sides?" he asked.

"She does not hate you."

"This baby . . . does she hate him the way she does Burgy?" He touched Mattie's hand beside him in the hay. "She swore off baby-making before he was born. Now she is two deep into disliking male babies."

Mattie caved her dress between her legs, setting her legs up in front of her like a man spitting tobacco between his knees. Her hair was long over the front of her shoulders, moving when she shook her head. "I don't think she hates Burgy, no, sir. She says this man is rich, bought her fancy clothes. Don't figure to me, the coming back if she was set to make that big a change and the coins too." Mattie looked up at Burley. "You think marriage was a chancre on her after seventeen years? Or is she just brought down by ordinary bedsores?"

"This farm's not a soft bed," he said.

"Hay can be comfortable." Mattie crumbled a hand of clovers. "If you don't make her eat it too."

"I never force-fed her."

"What do you call nine children then?"

"Eight."

"That baby is four months old."

Down the hill, framed in the door, the house waxed under the burden of sun and honey locust. Burley counted back, whistled a single note. A haze rose from the rear of the house.

"She's late in getting up the noon meal," he said.

"Maybe she learned four o'clock tea from this man and can't get the time straight," Mattie said.

"I don't figure," he said.

"Are you going to eat at the table with her?"

"She hasn't been home long enough to come out to

the barn and get up a pot of hay." He did not help her up. He looked at the smoke. "She don't even know how to cook it so it will look better than fodder."

———————

"IT'S ABOUT HALF AND HALF WITH THEM," DALIAH SAID, stacking plates. "Otho don't count. He can't even focus his eyes to see if you're not Cass. Carlene and Paul and John Jr. are on my side."

"And I got Burgy and Nathan and Silas."

"Mattie," she said.

"Mattie," he said.

Burley sat at the table still, over bony fish on yellow china, a glass of water, biscuits cut round by the glass she kept by the board, with peach jelly. He should have already pushed himself away when she reached for the dishes and put them in the water to soak. She took a drink from the gourd dipper by the sink, and came back to fold the tablecloth over the leftovers until supper. It was the closest she had been to him in a year. They had sat at opposite ends of the table during dinner as before. She brushed some crumbs into her hand. Some fell over his lap. He brushed them away and said,

"How can we do this? I don't get the facts. I don't get the reasoning."

"He'd been married once, didn't have no children to pass on the investment. I pitied him, I guess."

"I mean, how many times . . . I mean, did—"

"Like we was married," she said.

"So how can you be sure?"

Daliah wore a Florida dress. She had her apron tied high against the dishwater. Her dress was spotted anyway.

"Of course a baby was the last thing I needed." She

fingered the spots on her dress. "Doesn't matter how I know. Just matters that I am his mother. That's as close as knowing gets." She dropped her skirt. "I don't think it's ruint. Besides how can you know he ain't?"

"You'd think I would have built up my herd."

"Babies aren't no animals."

"Or maybe he was just a cull."

Daliah stepped close to Burley, closer than she had been to him in a year and a minute. "I tell you my running was because you gave me nothing. You saved me nothing."

"I've come up now," he said. Their faces were up to each other. New lines were around her eyes. She was older. "I have made good this year. I expect better next year."

"Better now. Better next! Why not better then?"

"How can you curse the past when you flaunt it? That baby. Them clothes." Burley moved from the table. It was afternoon, and he had not even thought about work, even as he talked of their work. "Flaunting, making me swallow when I'm not partial to the taste myself." He said, "It is not sweet."

"Then you won't," she said.

"I can't," he said.

She took off her apron. The dress was too far gone. She folded the apron once, then over itself, and hung it over the basin handle, so she was facing the window, looking out, and not at him and summertime coming.

"Will we still live in this house?"

"Now there's the problem," he said. "Eight babies still have to be fed. You can't rightly leave them new dependent on you again—or are you planning to vacation again this summer?"

"No," she said.

"Well, then, I by right have the mobility now. I

[153]

could leave, but for them eight babies I still got to plow, and could you think of a better place closer lived between dark and sunrise. I don't want to walk far." He cleared his throat. "I guess there is the barn."

"You needn't," she said. "We might as well work the appearance awhile."

"I promise you," he said.

"It's a big bed anyways."

"I said I promised," he said again.

BURLEY HAD THREE HOURS BEFORE SUNDOWN. HE WORKED far after dark honing his plow with a round rasp. Razz-cluck; razz-cluck, returning and striking. He could see through the open doors to the house, saw until the dusk quitted the walls. No one came for him at supper. He thought he saw Mattie in a rear doorway, looking toward the barn, but someone came behind her and Mattie moved away. He could not have seen if anyone was looking out for him now. He was not hungry.

He finished with the horse, currying her by kerosene light. He gave the animal a palm of dried apples, rubbing the flank, saying, "There now. There now. They's just apples." The horse snorted. "And you and me sure know from apples."

He thought to settle back into the straw for the night. After all he had done the same just the evening before. He even liked barns. He could have ridden the animal through the night, but he was kind and let the horse rest. He had not treated her kindly, taking her from the barn early yesterday morning and riding breakneck and almost across the family cemetery before he got the animal righted and quieted, and with Jaretta Chapel yelling at him about reading letters he had no addressed right to have read in the first place. He thought about the letter now, wished he had read it. But it was in his coat pocket, a night and a full day ready for him, unread, now draped across a kitchen chair (if Daliah had left his coat unhung, and had not retrieved and been astonished by the return to her hand of her own faults). Maybe if he had read it like Jaretta said, he would not have run up on the station late yesterday, saying: "Is there anywheres near where I can get hooked up to a train going south. I mean as far as Florida—all the way down?"

"Well, Florida is as far as you can go south."

"Ona," he said.

"What?" the clerk said.

"A train into Ona?"

"What's an Ona?"

The clerk pulled out a section schedule. Railroads passed into roundhouses, out of Lexington, and off the sides. "We're a small outfit here. We can route you over into Louisville, maybe," the clerk laid a pencil beside a black line hatched and crossed off the map. "Was a train. Transferred out of Atlanta, then Chattanooga, came in on the C & O line about six hours ago. There was freight from Florida on it. Not much, odd produce and such. A few passengers there was." The clerk closed the book. He laughed. "There was one gal off the train, dressed to the nines, carrying a chap with her under one arm which wasn't so bad, but"—he leaned over the counter—"she had one of those carpetbags. Was a rose-colored bag. Right out of place it was."

Burley came around the desk. "What was her name?"

"We don't take no names coming."

"Where did she go?"

"I gave her a route on a pass through. Nothing

regular where she was going. Harrodsburg was the closest. She showed me on the map where she wanted. Was just a spur off into Mercer County. I told her there was nothing but coal wagons and a number of timber procurers."

"Show me where. No, on the map what did she point out?" Burley dragged at the section maps. He saw Harrodsburg, and McAfee, and the curving blue line which was the Salt.

"She was near familiar with this section. Like she had pored over maps like this. Right up to where she was going. I never seen anything like it, a fine fanciful lady, talking and shoving like she was a man with a rightful mind done made."

"She left?"

"Five hours ago."

———

He stepped around the wicker chairs on the porch. In sunlight they would have made a latticework on the wall, and he could have climbed it. He climbed the lattice from memory into the tunnel of the breezeway. A cat crossed low and silhouetted on the back of the porch. Yellow eyes turned on him, turned to the side and out over the steps. He unlaced his boots and left them on the boardwork, finding as he stepped white-socked into their room something out of place. He saw his white feet moving too well and sure and familiar across the floor. He fell over the cradle set up in the niche between the door and the April window. The baby did not wake.

"Fool," she said.

"Sorry," he said.

He left his clothes in a pile beside the bed. The room was muggy. He reasoned she had not opened the

shutters because of the baby. The husk rolled. He lay
back on the bedding, taking a pillow between his head
and his hands, his back to her. She had thrown the covers
back. She was warm too. He twisted slightly to see her in
the dark. She was far to the other side of the bed. Three
feet of wasted muslin was between them. He fell over
onto his back, thinking, *Just so I gets my side. I just
wants the little I got coming.* He sweated and he wiped
his shoulder with the back of his hand. It was almost
like their first night.

It had been spring then, too, but not so warm. The
shutters had been opened, and the new locust looked cut
by scissors and pasted on slate. He thought back over the
day. (How his sister's hand had put white spirea in the
buttonhole of his black coat. His mother finished mending the hem of her church dress, biting off the thread.
She wore three petticoats he saw. He saw it all in her
face as she let the skirt drop, the six other sons, her man
dead, a green-eyed sadness now that her last son was
dying from her too. "What can I tell you," she said.
"Her mother's gone, can't tell her the woman things.
Your Pa dead, and Cletus too. No man to explain the
man things—no I don't need to know the fact. If you
have learned, I can't blush to hear you say." She
straightened his collar. She had large hands. "Seems I
should send you over there. Even if Ren Brownlee is a
drunk at least for sure he knows the hows. And I could
assure Daliah." She moved his flower. "I have always
liked spirea," she said. She wiped her green eyes. "I ask
that you be gentle and long suffering with her. She is of
deep hurts. And you are so kind," she said. "I'll try," he
said. "Yes, I do like spirea.") But the thinking was
dulled.

He intended that first night seventeen years before
to lay back until, stretching his bare legs and touching

the footboard. The wood had been cold. He did not look for her yet. She was small and off on the boundary to his right, and he must get it right, understand because they were new married and he knew. *What if she bleeds. She must bleed and I do not want her to bleed.* He churned his head into the pillow, seeing the hair loose and quivering over her forehead. *Did he tell her enough? For God! Did he tell her enough?*

"Do you want me to come over there," she said, "or do you want to meet in the middle?"

Touching her loosely, the hands placed then moving, and words left his mouth. He did not know what he said. He did not hear the words; he uttered them too low. And there was her face the first time, shining and new washed, the wedding flour was gone. Her let-down hair was between their chests, rolling like grit between bare breast and bare breast, and a stem of unretrieved baby's breath from behind her bride's combs splintered like fine pillow down in her hair. He tasted pale color as he bit at her, muttering the words without breaking between his teeth less he replace color with air, and lose her, taking in, and betraying her.

She had been just sixteen, no matter what her daddy had armed her. No matter he had asked eight—*no nine, she says nine now*—children from her and asked, received, and reared from her those man-children and two suffering daughters.

"Sorry," he said.

He held her hand in the dark. It was lifeless and small, and well-formed. Her high cheek was planed against the night window, cloudless, and unmired, and long suffered too.

"I said no," she said.

"Remind me to explain to you about them taxes sometime."

[158]

THE LAND WAS UNWASHED. THERE HAD BEEN NO RAIN in two weeks. As he plowed, again plowed, red earth powdered before the tines and settled, again settled. Daliah was like before. She wore a Florida dress, but then all she had were Florida dresses and she wore one carelessly at breakfast. She cooked in it, splashed bacon fat, and did not care. She asked about the plowing. Birds were plentiful in the fields. He roused two coveys with the blade and watched them scatter. He came across the field again, made the turn, hitching the mule twice on the flanks with the plow lines. "Up c'here," he said. The mule held furrow true, and from one end of the near field, back, forth, and turning, made less than effort with him. John Jr. was across the fences with another span in the river bottoms. Nathan and Paul hoed the kitchen garden. Mattie took Silas and Carlene and buckets to hunt early dew berries. Burley's mouth watered from their taste with cream.

He made the run at the far end of the fields, and saw her materialize out of the clay, small and not the same color as the ground. Her dress was blue this time, like the sky, in the far shadows of the trees. She had two pails. He moved up behind the mule, struggling because he had not seen her since breakfast, and after he had left their bed.

"I would not have hurt you," he said.

"I brought John Jr. his lunch too. Biscuits and ham and cold milk," she said.

"Makes him think he's a man."

"I wasn't worried about you taking me. I said the appearance. I said nothing for the fact."

He took a drink from the milk. It was cold and made his eyes hurt. He wiped his mouth with a forearm.

White rings were in his arm hair. The sun was already bright. "Mattie," he said.

"It will be Mattie who'll not let us forget."

"Jaretta Chapel?"

"Even Jaretta will quiet. She's more taken with you than in the past. You must have impressed her this year."

"I was a saint," he said.

"We must reconcile for the children. We are too old not to try to." She left John Jr.'s pail at her feet. It was not as large as Burley's. She had not planned for two men in the field. "I know. I tried."

He brought the milk down from his mouth again. There was a ring around his chin too. "You mean it's over, for sure over?"

Daliah was not wearing an apron. In strong light she was still handsome, and yes, the blue dress. She did not have her combs in. Her hair was gathered and tied in the back. "But look, Burl, I had a spark. I found a rich man living in a house that weren't always surrounded by corn. I could have had it."

"You were a fool to come back."

"I know it," she said.

"I learned to live without you. I could have done it, too."

"I know it," she said.

"I'm glad you're back," he said quickly.

Daliah raised a hand over her eyes, sighting across the fences. Burley thought she was looking for John Jr., but under the palm her gray eyes were on him. She was not smiling. "You won't be glad if we don't get it right this time," she said. "We have to get Mattie off the middle and down here among us."

Burley capped his milk. He put it back in the pail. "Well, then, you mind if I take this packing back up to the house? We might as well sit down and pretend it's all right now."

"I got more buttermilk in the well shed. It's cool too."

"Turned enough?"

"Right well I suspect."

"Maybe we can get Mattie to drink with us."

"She don't like buttermilk."

"Well, now," Burley said. He took the other pail from her too, putting them both in one hand, setting the buckets at right angles like lovers' hands held together. He took her hand. "By what we got to feed her she just might learn to like buttermilk to wash it down."

"John Jr.," she called across the fences.

They walked slowly back. The house drew fast upward and still unpainted. Burley thought, *That whitewash ought to take nice to them boards.* They crossed near the fence bordering the County Road. No one had traveled the road all morning. Yesterday's tracks were lifeless and suspended. No one might pass at all today. Maybe not tomorrow. Daliah cut them softly across the corner of the field. Burrs and sage brushed at their thighs. Queen Anne's lace stirred about their ankles. They came nowhere near the cemetery fence. Chickens roosted quietly under the shade of the porch. Burgess's cat came over the grassless yard. Its pawprints looked like pink shells among the great waves raked in the dust. Burgess squatted on the third step and worked at a knotted rope. Three chipped marbles were lined up and balanced on a crack between the boards. Red cat's eyes. Burley set down his pails and helped him with the hard part. Daliah said nothing. She just watched.

"There," Burley said. "Mind you keep it out now."

Burgess spoke up at them, not turning his mouth up to make the words plain at all. "You gave a whole thirty-five cents for Carlene's baby doll at Christmas, didn't you, Daddy? It was a whole thirty-five cents. I only got a dime for the new one. The man what took him said a dime was enough. Said he already paid Mama the balance."

Daliah even helped Burley onto the horse.

BIRDS FLASHED IN UNISON, SHOWING SILVER BREASTS LIKE dead fish bloated and belly up on a riverbank. Their flight was regular and pulsing, each turned and flashed as all turned and flashed even though they were scavengers and should have had no unity, thronging on decayed fruits, and seed corns, and manures. Burley's horse stepped awkwardly over the rails. Daliah had told him what to look for. The train had four cars, was painted brown, and no yellow lettering faded from its sides. The birds called and flashed overhead like seabirds who have followed rivers too far inland. They were only pigeons under a bright sun.

Caslin Krasavage sat behind his desk as Burley closed the door behind his back. The baby was unwrapped and lay with legs and arms moving in Caslin's lap.

"She did not even let me kiss the baby good-bye," Caslin said.

Burley laid his father-in-law's pistol on the ledge of the table.

"She didn't," Caslin said.

"She came back to me," Burley said. "She left you and came back to me."

The drapes on the far side had been drawn against the sun. The red-shaded lamp was lit, illuminating closed ledgers and a smooth-sanded baby's toy painted yellow. Burley stood eight feet farther away, listening to Caslin roll words out of his pale mouth, below pale waterless eyes, below pale yellow hair, circling the hard round words on his tongue.

"You have so many sons," Caslin said.

"She did come back to me, amd she brought this baby boy because she says he is mine."

"I could have stopped her," he said. "I have money. I can provide for him well."

Burley shuffled the carpet. "Yes," he said.

"You think she is a fool too," Caslin said.

"I told her so."

"I could fight you for him. I'm only forty-two."

"Why don't you offer to buy him from me?"

Caslin smiled. "You want cash money?" He opened a book of bank drafts. "Or do you want to trade me for the rest of the silk dresses Daliah left behind?"

"We don't have the closet room."

Caslin lifted the baby to the table. He folded the blanket over the child's legs. The baby kicked it off. Burley reached across to have the child, but Caslin blocked his hands.

"All right. All right, then," Caslin said. "What did she tell you to ask me for?"

Burley took his hand from under Caslin's. He passed over the pistol, featureless and loaded between them on the table. He could have reached for it. His hand did not slump to have it. There was the odor of drink, though no glass was set out. Caslin did not look drunk.

"Well now," Burley said. "Seems to look we might have some dickering."

"She never said she loved me," Caslin said. "But she never said she loved you neither."

"I thought we was talking about the money. I

thought we was talking why you couldn't buy her to staying on with you. Daliah's turned so easy by a store-bought package of hairpins or printed yard goods. You bought her dresses of real silk, and shiny leathers, and rouges, and glass brooches for her to wear on her bosom."

"Diamond," Caslin said.

Burley thought about that for a minute. "For sure now? And even for a true diamond you couldn't keep her?"

"Oh, but she still has the diamond. She could take a diamond with her. The house and the ranch and Florida she couldn't carry off. She even had to cut down on the dress goods to what she could balance off the baby in the other arm. Something as small as a diamond could not slow her."

Burley laughed. "But you can't be telling me this one whole year was just a shopping trip for her! That she was stuffing baubles in her carpetbag and down her dress front, and in the folds of the baby's blankets. God! That baby must have been a heartbreak. She had to waste a whole good arm just to pack it around."

"I bought her a trunk."

"It's a mile and a half from where the train dropped her off." Burley did not think of the gun. "And there's a good-size hill to make too."

"Yes, I know."

"Burgy thinks you cheated him."

"I should have given him a nickel too."

"No, thirty-five cents. He figures thirty-five cents."

Caslin brought up a glass from beside his chair. From eight feet it looked like bourbon. Burley shifted in his chair. *I can take him. He's not so different from me. I just got me seven sons to prove the point.* Out the

[164]

windows the birds flashed and beat wings one after and beside and among others. "First off," Burley said, "you give me a quarter for Burgy, and then we'll start."

TWO EMPTY GLASSES, ONE TIPPED OVER ON ITS SIDE, AND Burley leaned over the table, jabbing his hand hard against Caslin's chest. Burley's eyes were beaded and violent like bright sumac berries.

"When Silas was born I was sure we was done. I saw clear to the end when I would sit on my porch in the sundown and see my four sons come out of the field, bobbing right out of the dirt like they was another of my crops." Burley closed his eyes, they were red to him too. He did not wonder the drapes were drawn. It was a shock. "And there was a dreadful sense of failure in it, that a man's no more control over his babies, to have them come to him, to teach them, to love them in his best way, to see them as flawed copies of himself, as strangers because he had no more say in creating their texture than loose jism; and who can will their seed? Or plow under without destroying the earth under his feet?"

"You did not want sons?" Caslin said.

Burley had another drink. "Oh, but then there was the twins and Daliah clung too hard and killed Brett . . ." He had another sip. "She thought they was an omen to her from the first; and the morning I caught her throwing up dust in the summer yard, and she clung to him, dead, unconcerned about Carlene. I said to her when I prised Brett from her arms, 'What about Carlene?' not intending to slight Brett but he was another son and but another failure in my crop."

[165]

Burley wanted another drink but would not lift his glass, soiled and rank from bourbon, and too far down on the floor for him to reach now that he was drunk, to lift and fill behind his teeth before he could say to Caslin, "Dali did not think that lapse in Brett might have taken Carlene too, them being twins and bedded on the same sheets. She did not think that. She just didn't think that."

"I would sire a house of strangers then. I would me a lineage of failures like yours, Mead. I would." Caslin was a little drunk.

"I only wanted Carlene to be all right. That's all I meant by it."

"Daliah did not mean it that way," Caslin said. He tipped back his chair, swinging his feet up on the desk, and Burley's feet were there too, shod in work-ruined leather and April plow mire; and the gun.

"Is that why she deserted Burgy? Turned him out of her womb and said: 'God, another son and trial!'" Burley said. "Don't you see. I got to take on this new baby—Otho—because if I gave and took six, I got just the ease to take seven, and the seventh her only asking of the nine. If at all, she's to put Otho in Brett's place between Silas and Burgy, and right that one shame and grievance between us."

"So you got to have my baby."

"For such I leave call him Otho."

"Otho Haberstram Fox Krasavage."

"I can't go that Haberstram."

"It was my mother's family name."

"No, sir," Burley said. "Hardy. For my mother."

"Otho Hardy—Mead," Caslin said.

Caslin laid a cigar on his lower lip. The first match would not light. The second flared and Burley saw hands shake beneath its circle. *I've drunk too much*, he breathed.

"I don't smoke," he said.

Caslin put the second cigar back in the box and raised the gun in his retrieved hand. Burley was not frightened. He did not know if those old shells were any good. In eighteen years he had seen the gun fired only once. The gun lost shape in Caslin's manicured hands, appearing more a trophy among French cuffs, and grayspun. He seemed to be falling even before the gun discharged; and a shattering; he saw bourbon color as he floated down and the red carpet crushed against his face. He could not tell if it was his blood. *Maybe he's shot other men here too. This rug could have come off the loom woven white.* Something hard bit his back; his hand sounded it and rolled the whiskey glass from under his spine. The room did not spin. There was no pain, just the cool crush of the rug, the whiskey glass, and the chair legs somewhere about his head. The gun pointed at him again. *One of them shells might have been alive. I can't count the second will be good too.* The pistol turned butt end toward him.

Caslin said, "She's driving up. I'm sure she heard it. Take it."

Burley pulled himself up over the edge of the table. Caslin had shot the light out, the globe shattered inward, and the red shade crumpled over Caslin's unworked hand like blood.

"Is it my turn?" Burley said.

"She heard it. We must not let her think you did not achieve honor." Caslin gathered the baby from the chair where he had placed him, kissed him lightly on the head, and gave him across. He tucked the yellow toy in the folds of the blanket.

"Don't for a minute think I wouldn't still fight you for him," Caslin said. "And I lied. I was forty-three last week."

———

The train was moving even before he stepped down from the rear car. The baby lay in his great arms, covered and downy haired under the sun. The birds flashed and blinded him.

Daliah stood down. She had changed her dress, a bright and showy frock. Jaretta Chapel was drawn up in her carriage beside her. Daliah looked white though she had not had time to place her powders above her cheeks.

"You shot him," she said.

He weighed the gun. He thought to hand it over to her (perhaps it was her turn again); he had carried it seventeen years now, had carried and vainly deposited silt: passage and marriage and regeneration and failure and loss and work and redemption and abandonment and trial and heart were piled on, swirling and singing like tuneless white-bellied birds. He tested the weight of the new baby in his other arm. It was not so great. *By God, wouldn't she have been killed to see me step down if he'd been triplets.* And only the gun was foolish.

He pocketed it.

"I said I would buy my own shells," he said.

CHAPTER SEVEN

NOVEMBER

1963

THE SMOKEHOUSE FLOOR WAS LITTERED WITH HOT white onions. Soup beans boiled outside on an open brick furnace. Otho handed down a worm-pocked ham, wrapped in some burlaps and tied in festering twine.

"We'll trim it up fine," Otho said. "Hams all look like such before they get to the table."

Coming out of the shed their breath rose higher, frost columns, then dispersed. He followed behind again, wagging the twelve pounds of meat and cloth in his arms. The grandfather's hands were red. He unlatched the door to the cellar.

Jars shone like prisms throwing inward fruit-lights about in shades of gooseberry green, damson mauve, peach amber. Three sacks of potatoes spilled out of a corner. Otho snapped an overhead cord, electricity jumped, and the mason jars sang: gooseberry jade, damson crimson, peach gold. Otho carelessly trod one potato under his heel, reaching over to finger a row of jars, pushing some back, drawing another forward. "She said there was one more apricot preserve '59." He pushed another jar out of the way. "Her memory is getting wishful." Otho turned to another shelf.

The ham was heavy. It bled on his hands.

"She'll have to settle for peaches 1961." Otho pocketed the quart jar in one side of his great coat. He turned back and got a jar of stewed tomatoes. It went into the opposite pocket and he was balanced.

Otho banked the fire. No odor rose against the late November wind. The grandson blinked twice coming up out of the earth though there was no sun; through squinted eyes he saw his grandfather clothed in wood smoke and breath-frost, and the colorless sky flattened behind him and the birch trees too melted in the cold. The mason jars clinked in Otho's pockets as he worked at the fire, or when he walked, rounding the house and up one step, clink, one step, clink onto the rear porch.

Otho spoke again. "Was not a photograph taken of my face until I was twenty-seven years old. Was when your Uncle Will, Dison's brother, came back from the war. In 1918, October, we was gathered. I was married then, six years, had me two babies; they's in the picture too. In the closet somewheres." Otho leaned back. "Daliah is in the picture too. She died five months later. It was the last picture taken of her."

He trimmed fat from the ham. Otho threw the slabs onto wax paper, letting them plop like packed pails of sand. They were in a back room off the kitchen, unheated, and cluttered with details: a freezer, stacks of out-of-town newspapers in twine, a box of lye soap cut in wedges like chocolate cake, coconuts shipped from a son in Florida, rolled linoleum printed with pale rose garlands, funeral fans and Easter baskets hanging on nails from the walls.

He pointed the hock-billed knife at his grandson. "She was a fine woman. I heard some bad words spoke among the neighbors, from my own wife, saying and whispering about my birth. I lived in my mama's and daddy's protection." He cut at the ham again, cutting deep for a worm. "It might not have been love; it was at

[172]

least safe." He had a stiff mound of fat on the sheet of wax paper. He wiped and put away the knife, snapping it shut quickly with a little flourish. "Whispering don't change pride in a name one comes to bear. I am a Fox or Folsom or such too."

"Why was I named Samuel?"

Otho shoved the hog fat across. "Who would name their son Otho?" he said. "Take this out and drop it in the beans. Makes a nice soup."

HE SAT BETWEEN THEM AGAIN, AND MEMORY STRETCHED wrinkled like the oilcoth; valleys of orange crumb cake, unboiled sassafras roots laid out like yellow stained and stunted hands, and cellophaneless candies. Otho ate chicken hearts and livers and craws.

Samuel pushed his plate away. A shank bone rattled from his plate as his grandmother raked the scraps into a galvanized pail for the dog. He reached for one more biscuit, overcooked and powdered with flour across the top. His grandfather was having the last of his coffee, Maxwell House, he called it, the Loving Cup Coffee (pointed a jointed finger at the good-to-the-last-drop). With his coffee he ate vanilla wafers ("The best little cake in the world," he even said), taking the coffee without cream, no sugar. The table linen was oilcloth. Otho had not ceased talking during the meal. Heat from the stove softened the listening, like wax, catching dust and thoughts like insects in tar resins.

"He would not have whispered it in her ears if he had said," Dison said.

"What could he have done but forgive her?" Otho said.

Otho poured his coffee into a saucer to cool. He

drank it in sips. Dison Jane swirled the ice in her tea (even in winter she took ice in her tea; swirling was her hobby). One forearm lay across her stomach cupping her side. She rested her other elbow on the perch, the arm swung out like a fish gaff, swirling her ice. She listened closely, indignantly.

"He was sixty-four years old. You can't mean he would waste them sixty-four years to say, 'I'm sorry and I love you.'" She wrenched back the handle of the ice tray. Splinters flew and melted fast under the lips of bowls. She put seven cubes in her glass. When she poured her tea it was white from the ice.

My bicycle's on the porch. I will be home by seven, Samuel thought. *She didn't give me any ice.*

"She was on her deathbed, Dison," Otho said. "He could not have said it loud. He never told her before."

"No. I'm going to have milk instead. I don't need any ice," Samuel said.

Dison put the other tray back in the freezer. "And told her what? He was in her ear for minutes. I-love-you is three words. I'm-sorry makes five."

"I was at the window. I did not hear."

"Loni was in my lap. I couldn't get up fast enough to see more than her lips move twice. Daliah said, 'It's a funny thing.'" The ice had not melted enough for Dison to swirl.

If I leave now I can be home by six-thirty, he thought.

The milk was not cold. Samuel did not like chicken parts. He ate shelled beans, almost the whole jar of stewed tomatoes Otho had brought from the cellar, and hard potatoes. Old people food. He had never seen Dison make potato salad. He wanted but did not reach for cereal; a box of Corn Flakes was tipped over on the refrigerator, its red and green feathered cock cawing

[174]

sideways into the strawberries and trademark bowls. There would be ice cream in gallons if he wanted.

"You saying Mama made fun of my daddy?"

"And her face painted white like a clown."

"It was just a little corn flour."

"Was she a bakery good?" Dison said.

Strings of dried pepper pod on the wall behind him framed Otho's head. Dison laid a hand on his across the table.

"I mean the man that seduced her with the odor of sweet cottons, stephanotis blossoms, and the stench of soft living," Otho said. "You did not know the story. I married you in the spring of 1911 when Mama and Daddy were old and tired. I breathed the air from their lungs when life was still in them."

Dison slowed her ice. "Listen to him brag." She moved a box across to Samuel. "Have some of these vanilla cakes before Otho chokes on them and the crumbs."

Samuel took a wafer between his teeth. It was very sweet.

"She was my mama," Otho said.

"And John Burley was your daddy."

"I can hope," Otho said.

"There ain't none of the man's money in it."

"I wasn't imagining money inheritance to the boy."

Over the vaporless leftover ham and shelled green beans, Otho was quiet, and Dison's ice had melted and given up, finished its whirled and watered tea, diluted and pink.

Dison turned on Samuel. "Did he offer you money?"

Samuel smiled. "Three dollars."

"Thirty-five cents," Otho said. "Three dollars and thirty-five cents."

[175]

"No, you got to subtract the thirty-five cents," Samuel said. "Two dollars and sixty-five."

"Did you promise him compound interest for the seventy-one years?"

"Three percent," Otho said.

"It's a joint account!"

Samuel cut them off. "Leave them alone," he said. "Just leave them alone."

WHEN A BABY, HIS HANDS CRAWLED THE NEW LINOLEUM grasping in his fists surprised air when the raspberry-patterned laurels would not leave the floor. Above the legs of cane chairs gathered about Sunday shoes, relatives handed down to him and cousins squirrel legs, and he sucked their juice, and was given in turn soft peppermint down from the alcove whiteness of the floured cutting boards. He learned to climb the cabinet. His knees were white. In the kitchen he ate yellow ice custard and Nabisco Vanilla wafers, sucking on them at his chair between the basin and the refrigerator, opening the door to have milk and orange ring cake. Fish came down from the freezer in milk-carton blocks. Bloody headless perch floated in stewing pans to thaw and fry. Otho snapped white-feathered chicken necks with an overhand flip, the head cawing in his hand while the living body ran and pumped rust-iron blood among the dandelions and bee clovers. Pin feathers eddied in hot water around his mother's complaining hands. A chicken claw opened and closed on a roost. In summer he ate fried dried apple foldovers in front of a box fan propped between the kitchen door and the back room, drawing the heat down from the ceiling and into the twined newspapers, and lye soap wedges, and dry-cleaning hangers chattering like chimes; when a baby.

So he did not know if the letter was a lie. Even if Otho had told him. "You think one match couldn't burn them pages," for all the gospel his grandfather had said. He had read the letter for the third time, following the brown ink and wishing Daliah Faye was writing again at that very table, and that he could stop her hand and say, "What do you mean by this?" He imagined her in white cotton and hair tied in grosgrain ribbons. Belief could have been set aside, or better buried in the iris and cosmos, for then what Dison had said would have been manure. Rag paper made good mulch.

Samuel could see her hand the first time he had read:

March 23, 1893
Dearest Jaretta,

I feel like just writing and explaining what has happened, but that would be unfair. It's been months since I see you, talked, confided—needed you.

I've been running ever since April last, even when I was in bed resting I was hurrying too, and here I am in Florida. I am right this minute sitting in Florida writing to my best friend trying to tell you what I haven't reckoned to myself.

Jaretta, don't hate me. I know you think I'm dread for running out on Burley the way I did and all, and leaving him with seven childrens, and Mattie, the oldest, having to fend off the other six children and her father just to get supper on the table. But I knew you'd be over the minute I was gone to help out, to see if

Carlene and Burgess and Silas was dressed better than Burley would even consider covering them, like they was never to be see by another living body except the other children and him, and you, Jaretta. And I'm sorry, but Burley never likened onto you much, thought you was a nosey woman just trying to learn gossip from the original source, but I knowed you'd be watching my children from a distance, looking over every fence on the place to see if they was right put up. I even believed you'd walk up and down the County Line Road four times a day to see between the mimosa if Mattie was able to get the wash straight clipped to the clothesline. I'll make it up to her, Jaretta. You see—Mattie being fifteen and you being you was my only pins on leaving Burley that way. With the both of you standing up to him I'd know Burley wouldn't have the disposition to talk about me in front of the other children. I couldn't have took the leaving knowing he was poison on me to the little ones. But then I should have known Burley would not have said. He never said before, and now I might as well admit right out in front of you here on this paper how I may have wronged him in my thinking. I never once heard his word against me. I thank him for that. After Brett died he never asked as if I might have been at fault for favoring on him too much. I couldn't tell him to stand back from the porch so I could see to the cemetery the way I needed to. I couldn't ask him to get down off the step because he was in the way of me walking over to the plot to take up the weeds. But you know I was terrified because once Brett left me, then another of them might of too, and if once then once again, then all of them might. Burl let me run up on you, Jaretta, even though he was my husband and ought to have been hearing the fears I mouthed like prayers into your ears.

Not to say I don't worship you, I trust you like my god. And maybe that's how I can confess this sad storytelling like I was some fault-finding Episcopalian needing your grace to carry on out the door again. Burley couldn't have stood the thinking I would have laid out on you. That's why I left! He couldn't have been quiet long enough to let my words ring in his ears that way. Your head would have chimed like a bell. Ring for me, Jaretta, I need to have you ringing and ringing for me as I come back. I am coming back. That's why I have to tell you, to set me up. Let Burl know.

But how can I? You wouldn't believe where I've been, have seen, had done to me in these months. There was this man, see, and in the beginning he gave to me and I was giving back to him. And Jaretta, hear! Chime loud for me now —I have lain with this man! Forgive me. I said it too fast. It happened too fast for me to remember details, the train, the hotel—a hotel in Tampa, Florida with arches and domes and rich folks dancing on the grass lawn in the middle of the day like there weren't an acre of ground that needed plowing anywheres in America! I have drunk French champagne, Jaretta. It's pale, right flat compared to Daddy's corn or fox grape. But I like it, and having lain with this man I birthed again.

Your head must have tolled like the twin

bells in the Willow Grace Baptist Church! Temper them awhile longer because I have to strike at them again.

He is my seventh son, Jaretta. We have named him Otho. He has green eyes. He was born in December and you can count on your fingers as well as I can. I can't think about the chances. What might be the truth I give to them green eyes. Jaretta, I count the very days and the possibility—even hours. That's why I'm coming home. The man knows too.

I didn't tell you! He is a rich man. Think of it. I birth a namesake heir in the home of a wealthy man—me who never saw seventy dollars at one time without thinking of redoing all the curtains in that house of Burl's and rugs and winter shoes for the children.

And that's why I run too. I couldn't think about them kids walking County Line Road with cold winter shoes. Burl was no help in it. Money was his saving grace. He never had enough to tempt me to staying forever with him. And security was all I ever wanted. I fear of knowing tomorrow more powerful than any fear I know. It makes me mad that fairness is thrown out to them that get the chance to buy onto it like fairness was dry goods too long left on the shelf and put on sale to rid the store of the rotten smell of fading percale.

You know what money'll do for you? I'll tell you, Jaretta, me who sits here writing to you on hand-'graved stationery and with a diamond brooch of my own on my breast. Money is good only for shoving away the fears of fighting everybody for the chance to buy onto that dry goods fairness. That's called investment, and what this man Cass calls annuity, and "fudu-ci-ary" such. That's what this man can offer me, an investment in dry goods fairness that wouldn't make a decent run up of curtains because I could never decide where to cut off the material and make a seam.

See, I'm not so terribly dread. It's not like being dead, I told myself. Like I was gone from you and the family, buried beside Brett knowing weren't be no one but you, Jaretta, who'd ever pass by to see if the foxtail and jimson was growing on my grave. You wishing you could step in there just one afternoon a season to clean away the weeds to read what lettering Burley might rightly decide was proper over a woman who gave him eight children, supper on the table, and some distance across the bed for him to reach over. The fading letters would probably say: Dali Mead gave a fine litter. How can you bury what never been alive? I told you I lived some right up to the minute I was writing this letter, in this house, this rich man's house that raises up from the ground and is no more cared after than cornfield peas scattered between the row— that same pea color, paintless until I stepped up and declared on it as if it was my hand what carried nail and board, but missed the brush. I was just scared, and when I'm scared I say much what ought never been mouth. But I was without words, saying stupid things and taking nigh until July to tell him I was having this baby. I bed with him because I believed I was not good for else, that I was a body of a harlot for him to father a man-child. It scared me, Jaretta. But it

was no different than my others, waking up sixteen years ago and having Mattie in my arms,
like the other seven children were lost in this
one great birthing that took me sixteen years to
breathe air into the lungs of this boy we have
named Otho. And this time you weren't there.
You, Jaretta, who stood at most every one of my
babies, beside the bedstead holding my hand,
and in kindness allowed me to do the same for
you when your Mathew, and Shem, and Prissy
was born. I had a nurse this time. She did not
hold my hand once.

Cass claimed onto this child like he was
God-given to him, fussing and telling how the
world was going to be his and all. I couldn't tell
him right out he was just another baby, weren't
no Allmighty achievement for me and him to
make a union and have this baby. And I wasn't
about to tell him the world weren't in no way
connected up with this child.

Jaretta, oh Jaretta, hear me! I'm saying
against Cass like I was married to him. Chiding
him on pretensions when in fact he was offering
me and my child the very claims I would have
made on him, to have the time to sit without
struggling, breathe pure airs under trees without
worrying of the wind storming and pushing up
corn just nigh high to stand up and be corn. Was
I wrong for wanting the respite? Don't you see,
Jaretta?

All right then. All right. I can't myself accept you seeing. I want to put down the burden,
some laying down of the fair investment. And
not just for tomorrow, but the tomorrow after—
tomorrow when I come home, I might wish, the

instant I sit to write this letter, I wish a host of my family and my one good friend like you, Jaretta, will be waiting to pull me in from this floodless river I've paddled from one bank to the other finding levees thrown too high up on either shore. Pull me off this river water, Jaretta, set up my return by simply telling Burl without hating me. If I have whored, I whored for a reason. And you are not the only one who would call me a prideful whore named desire.

Dali

NOW IT WAS SEVEN AND HE HAD NOT MOVED. HIS BICYCLE was unlifted from the porch, to come down onto the hard grass where his ghosts stirred, where in other seasons rotting crab apples stained his shoes pink, where he rooted june bugs beneath elephant ears twisting like white aluminum dishes in the sun. Inside June nights smoldering rags drove away mosquitoes and dragonflies and gnats; even fireflies drifted randomly far from the smoke under the shells of cherry blossoms. He did not want to ride from them yet. Now it was November and the air was washed cold and breathless and silver and defeated under autumn thunder which was vain and puny-sounding like water over small stones; a regular sweet mother.

The garden was inside now; Dison had quitted her beds and trellis and brick borders for the winter. He breathed above her kitchen jungle; clay pots were foil-wrapped; the red bells of Jerusalem Cherry rang off-key; brown thirty-year-old cactus was staked to broom handles with cotton strips like curls in a girl's hair; Wandering Jew was fragile around the iron cage where budgies nested; coat-of-many-colors bloomed in scraped turtle shells colored like faience; missing were lilies, funeral asphodels . . .

. . . holding lilies; his November-colored hands were knuckle up on the after-dinner oilcloth, washed at the basin and tea-bathed in orange cake color: Otho-stained and Dison-stained he had thought, but he was now Daliah-stained and Burley-stained and unnamed Fox-stained. He had not meant to spend the day, and tomorrow was school and different learning; holding lilies.

By the window and its glasslike plastic curtaining Daliah Faye Brownlee was shrouded in white flour and scattered wheat dust as she walked, spilling strong-voiced hymns among the crisp balls of dried hydrangea, and John Burley Mead with silver hair cut high above his ears called her coming around the porch, passing the small heads of Samuel's great-aunts and the six uncles ("No, seven, he said seven, he had a brother named Brett"), stepping downward into Mercer County dust under mimosa and locust and August rotting pears. A splintering of wooden eaves layered in hair; red names painted in youth; faces strobed between porch slats where hands were raised and were kissed; hams bled among violet and maroon mason jars; an envelope lettered in brown ink gave fast up into his hands names and burdens and fairness and percale breath, closed, reread, closed.

("I will not choose," he said. Otho passed by the door, looked in. "It will be eight before I get home. I will not choose!")

And he delivered it to the shelf, high up, no postage due, among the orange ring cake, chewing gum, and soft peppermint.